W9-AWL-775

Disney · PIXAR

AND

A Welcome/Ocular Book

Visit www.disneyeditions.com, a part of the GO Network

Eyenovels™ are coproduced by Welcome Enterprises, Inc. and Ocular Books.
Eyenovels™ logo design by Gregory Wakabayashi

Conceived by Roger Warner

Edited and designed by Roger Warner and H. Clark Wakabayashi

For Disney Editions, Editorial by
Ken Geist, Wendy Lefkon, Rich Thomas

The producers would like to thank the following people for their support:

From Pixar: Leeann Alameda, Ash Brannon, Ed Chen, Bill Cone, Kathleen Handy, David Haumann, John Lasseter, Jim Pearson, Katherine Sarafian, Lee Unkrich, Clay Welch
and
From Disney: Eric Huang, Tim Lewis, Carson Van Osten, Deborah Hayes

Library of Congress Cataloging-in-Publication Data on file.

FIRST EDITION
Printed in The United States of America
1 3 5 7 9 10 8 6 4 2

Disney • PIXAR

# TOY STORY

things were happening in Andy Davis's house...
WELL, WHAT DO YOU THINK?
OH, THIS LOOKS GREAT, MOM! CAN WE LEAVE THIS UP TILL WE MOVE?
SURE, BUT HURRY UP. YOUR FRIENDS ARE GOING TO BE HERE ANY MINUTE!
Moving day was coming up fast...and Andy's birthday party was about to BEGIN!
IT'S PARTY TIME, WOODY! YA-HOO!
YOU'RE MY FAVORITE DEPUTY!
ZZZZZZIP!
REACH FOR THE SKY!
SEE YA LATER, WOODY!

Andy *loved* his toys.
PULL MY STRING. THE PARTY'S *TODAY??*
And they loved him back... more than he *knew!*
*OKAY, THE COAST IS CLEAR! STAFF MEETING, EVERYONE!*
*EVERYBODY HEAR ME?* GREAT! OKAY, FIRST ITEM TODAY...HAS EVERYONE PICKED *A MOVING BUDDY?*
DO WE HAVE TO *HOLD HANDS?*
OH, YEAH, YOU GUYS THINK THIS IS *A BIG JOKE!* WE'VE ONLY GOT ONE WEEK LEFT BEFORE THE MOVE! I DON'T WANT ANY TOYS LEFT BEHIND.

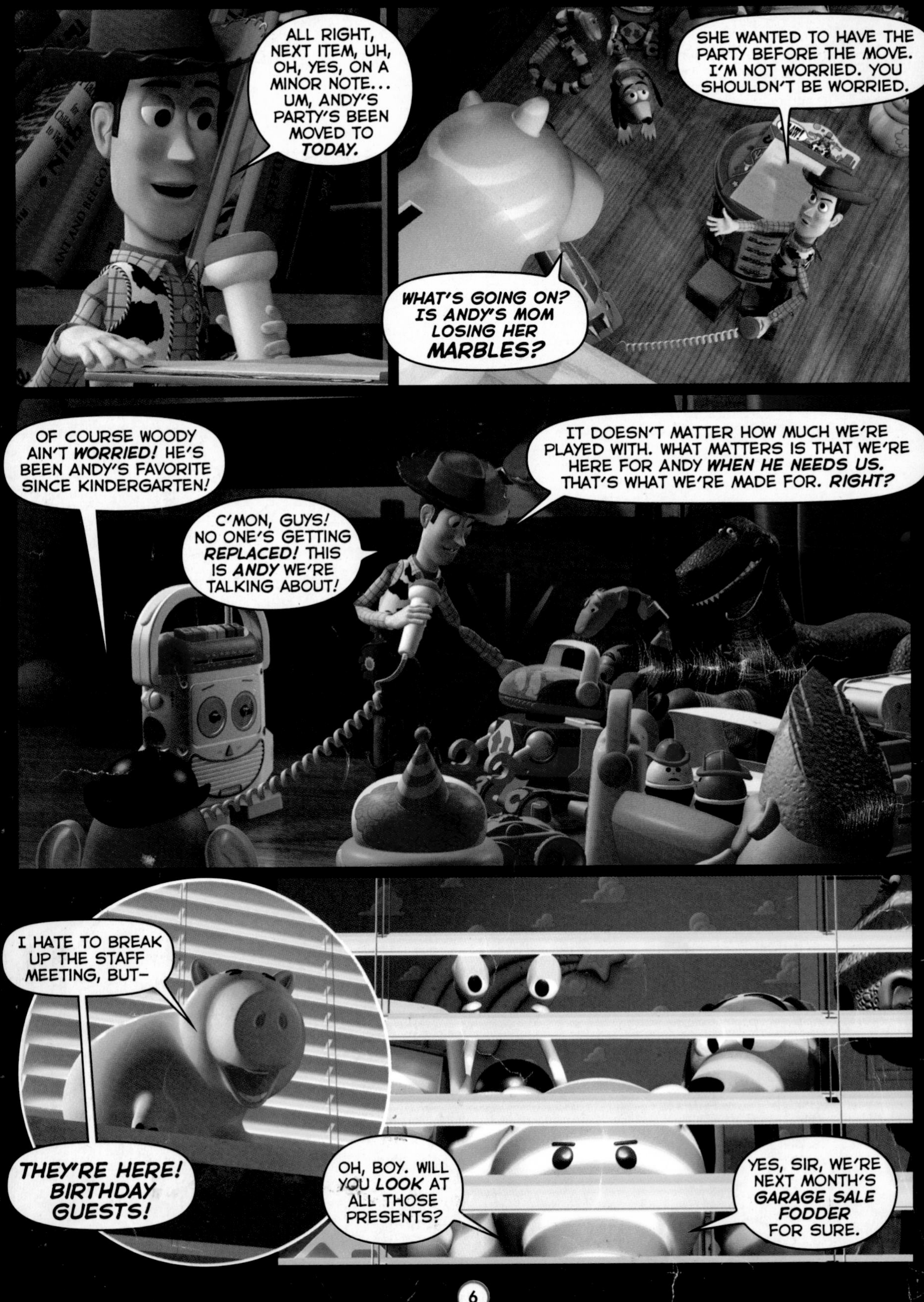
ALL RIGHT, NEXT ITEM, UH, OH, YES, ON A MINOR NOTE... UM, ANDY'S PARTY'S BEEN MOVED TO TODAY.
WHAT'S GOING ON? IS ANDY'S MOM LOSING HER MARBLES?
SHE WANTED TO HAVE THE PARTY BEFORE THE MOVE. I'M NOT WORRIED. YOU SHOULDN'T BE WORRIED.
OF COURSE WOODY AIN'T WORRIED! HE'S BEEN ANDY'S FAVORITE SINCE KINDERGARTEN!
C'MON, GUYS! NO ONE'S GETTING REPLACED! THIS IS ANDY WE'RE TALKING ABOUT!
IT DOESN'T MATTER HOW MUCH WE'RE PLAYED WITH. WHAT MATTERS IS THAT WE'RE HERE FOR ANDY WHEN HE NEEDS US. THAT'S WHAT WE'RE MADE FOR. RIGHT?
I HATE TO BREAK UP THE STAFF MEETING, BUT–
THEY'RE HERE! BIRTHDAY GUESTS!
OH, BOY. WILL YOU LOOK AT ALL THOSE PRESENTS?
YES, SIR, WE'RE NEXT MONTH'S GARAGE SALE FODDER FOR SURE.

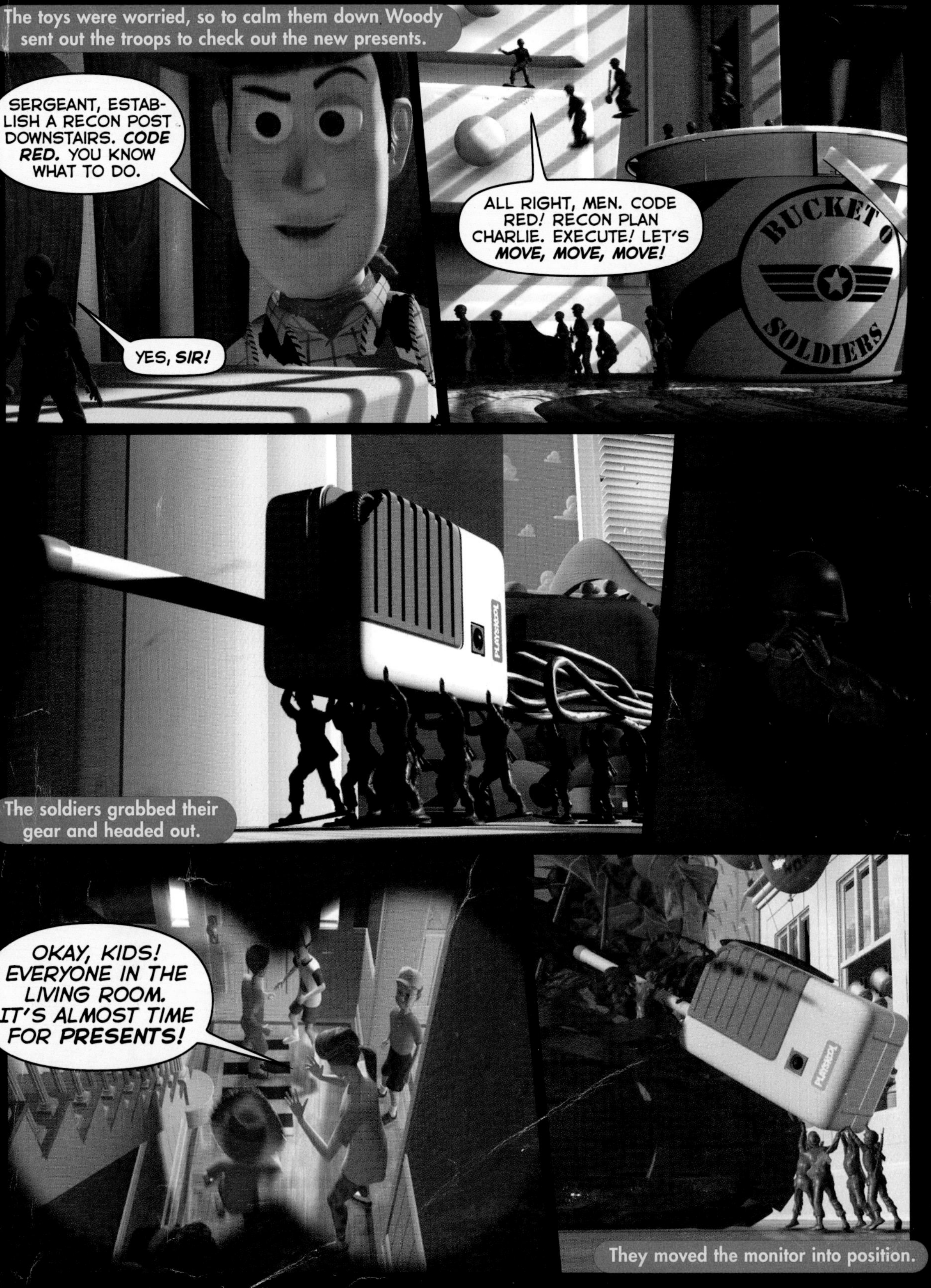

The toys were worried, so to calm them down Woody sent out the troops to check out the new presents.

SERGEANT, ESTABLISH A RECON POST DOWNSTAIRS. ***CODE RED.*** YOU KNOW WHAT TO DO.

YES, ***SIR!***

ALL RIGHT, MEN. CODE RED! RECON PLAN CHARLIE. EXECUTE! LET'S ***MOVE, MOVE, MOVE!***

The soldiers grabbed their gear and headed out.

*OKAY, KIDS! EVERYONE IN THE LIVING ROOM. IT'S ALMOST TIME FOR* ***PRESENTS!***

They moved the monitor into position.

In a panic, the toys all scattered around the room and then went back to their places—exactly the way Andy had left them.

The kids charged into the room...and then dashed out just as fast, slamming the door behind them.

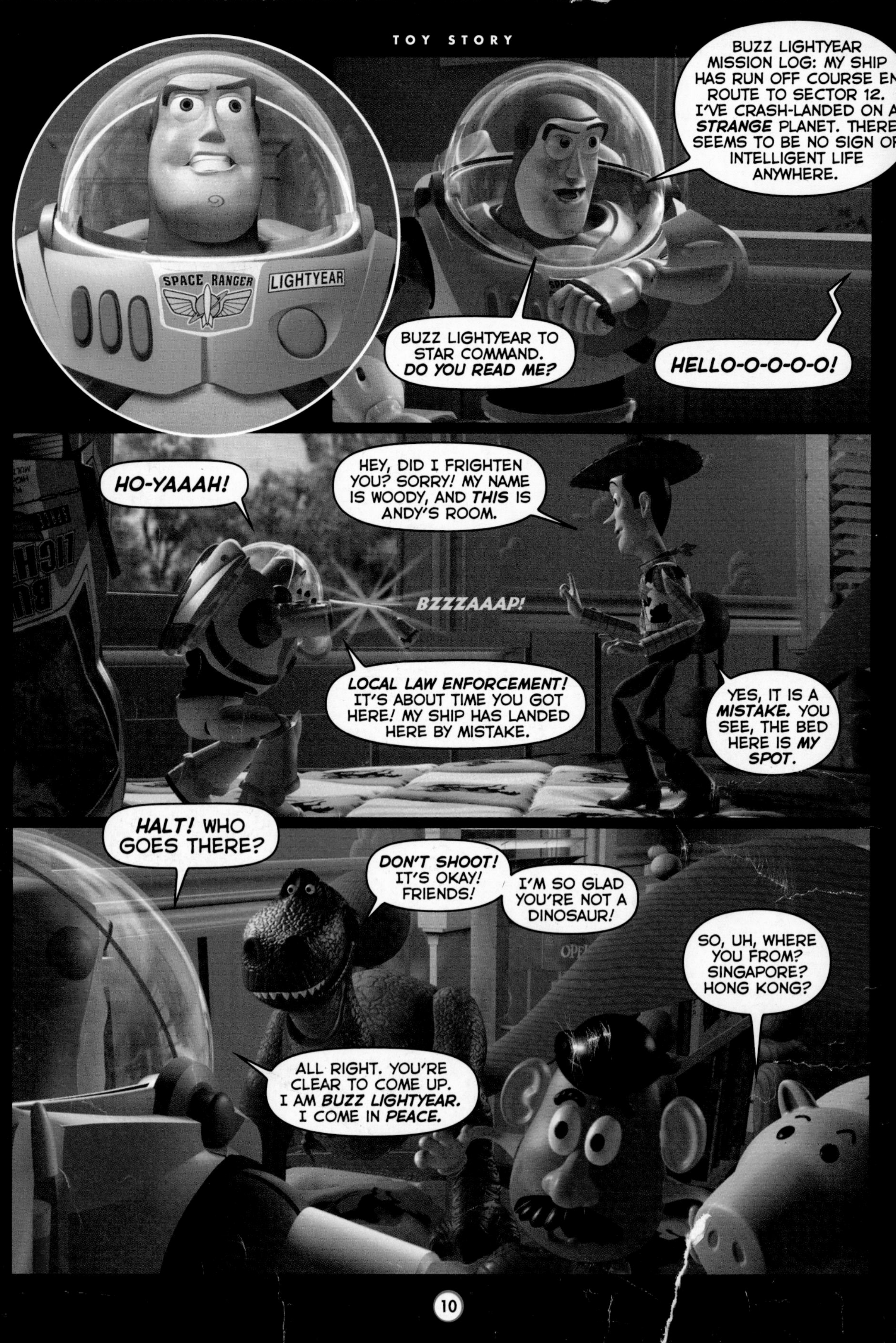
SPACE RANGER
LIGHTYEAR
BUZZ LIGHTYEAR MISSION LOG: MY SHIP HAS RUN OFF COURSE EN ROUTE TO SECTOR 12. I'VE CRASH-LANDED ON A *STRANGE* PLANET. THERE SEEMS TO BE NO SIGN OF INTELLIGENT LIFE ANYWHERE.
BUZZ LIGHTYEAR TO STAR COMMAND. *DO YOU READ ME?*
*HELLO-O-O-O-O!*
*HO-YAAAH!*
HEY, DID I FRIGHTEN YOU? SORRY! MY NAME IS WOODY, AND *THIS* IS ANDY'S ROOM.
BZZZAAAP!
*LOCAL LAW ENFORCEMENT!* IT'S ABOUT TIME YOU GOT HERE! MY SHIP HAS LANDED HERE BY MISTAKE.
YES, IT IS A *MISTAKE.* YOU SEE, THE BED HERE IS *MY SPOT*.
*HALT!* WHO GOES THERE?
*DON'T SHOOT!* IT'S OKAY! FRIENDS!
I'M SO GLAD YOU'RE NOT A DINOSAUR!
SO, UH, WHERE YOU FROM? SINGAPORE? HONG KONG?
ALL RIGHT. YOU'RE CLEAR TO COME UP. I AM *BUZZ LIGHTYEAR.* I COME IN *PEACE.*

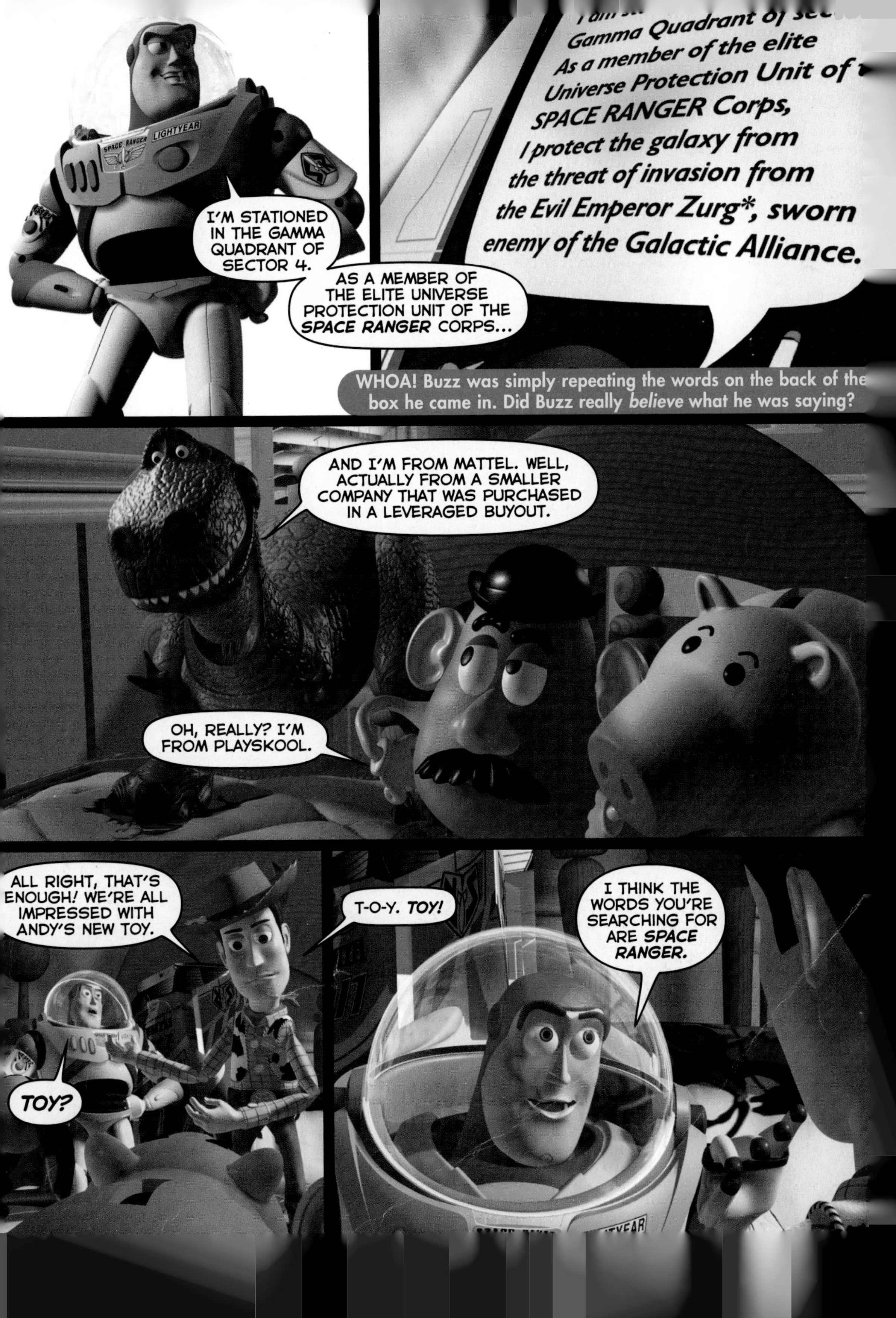

I'M STATIONED IN THE GAMMA QUADRANT OF SECTOR 4.
AS A MEMBER OF THE ELITE UNIVERSE PROTECTION UNIT OF THE *SPACE RANGER* CORPS...
Gamma Quadrant of
As a member of the elite
Universe Protection Unit of
SPACE RANGER Corps,
I protect the galaxy from
the threat of invasion from
the Evil Emperor Zurg*, sworn
enemy of the Galactic Alliance.
WHOA! Buzz was simply repeating the words on the back of the box he came in. Did Buzz really *believe* what he was saying?
AND I'M FROM MATTEL. WELL, ACTUALLY FROM A SMALLER COMPANY THAT WAS PURCHASED IN A LEVERAGED BUYOUT.
OH, REALLY? I'M FROM PLAYSKOOL.
ALL RIGHT, THAT'S ENOUGH! WE'RE ALL IMPRESSED WITH ANDY'S NEW TOY.
*TOY?*
T-O-Y. *TOY!*
I THINK THE WORDS YOU'RE SEARCHING FOR ARE *SPACE RANGER*.

WHAT DOES A SPACE RANGER ACTUALLY *DO?*
HE'S *NOT* A SPACE RANGER! HE DOESN'T FIGHT EVIL OR SHOOT LASERS OR FLY.
ARE PLASTIC. *HE CAN'T FLY!*
POP!
POP!
I *CAN* FLY!
CAN'T!
CAN!
CAN'T! CAN'T!
I COULD FLY AROUND THIS ROOM *WITH MY EYES CLOSED!*
OKAY, THEN, MR. LIGHTBEER, *PROVE IT!*
Buzz climbed the bedpost and jumped!
TO INFINITY... AND *BEYOND!*
BOING!
WOOOOOP!

ZZZZOOOOOOOOM!
WHUMP!
CAN!
THAT WASN'T FLYING!
THAT WAS FALLING— WITH STYLE!
BUZZ LIGHTYEAR
WOW, YOU FLEW MAGNIFICENTLY!
MAN, THE DOLLS MUST REALLY GO FOR YOU! CAN YOU TEACH ME THAT?
I FOUND MY MOVING BUDDY!

Soon Woody found his whole world had changed...
TO INFINITY AND BEYOND
BUZZ LIGHTYEAR
Was he being *replaced*?
IT LOOKS AS THOUGH I'VE BEEN ACCEPTED INTO YOUR CULTURE.
WELL, I MUST GET BACK TO REPAIRING MY SHIP.
*LISTEN*, LIGHTSNACK, YOU STAY AWAY FROM ANDY. *HE'S MINE*, AND NO ONE IS TAKING HIM AWAY FROM ME.
WHAT ARE YOU *TALKING* ABOUT?
SPACE RANGER
LIGHTYEAR
AND ANOTHER THING—*STOP* WITH THIS *SPACEMAN* STUFF! IT'S GETTING ON MY *NERVES*.

ARE YOU SAYING YOU WANT TO LODGE A COMPLAINT WITH *STAR COMMAND?*
YOU WANT TO DO IT *THE HARD WAY*, HUH?
DON'T EVEN *THINK* ABOUT IT, COWBOY.
RARF RARF
Everyone wondered what all the noise was about.
UH-OH.
*IT'S SID!*
YESSS! AH-HA HA-HA!
RARF
I THOUGHT HE WAS AT SUMMER CAMP.
THEY MUST HAVE KICKED HIM OUT EARLY THIS YEAR!
WHAT'S GOING ON?
NOTHING THAT CONCERNS YOU *SPACEMEN*. JUST US *TOYS*.
I'D BETTER TAKE A LOOK ANYWAY.
*AH-HA-HA-HA!*
WHY IS THAT SOLDIER STRAPPED TO AN *EXPLOSIVE* DEVICE?

YES! HE'S GONE! HE'S HISTORY!
THAT'S SID.
HE TORTURES TOYS– JUST FOR FUN!
I WANT YOU TO JOIN SPACE RANGERS
BOOM!

I'M GOING TO TEACH THAT BOY A LESSON.
WHAT ARE YOU DOING? GET DOWN FROM THERE!
I COULD HAVE STOPPED HIM!
BUZZ, I WOULD LOVE TO SEE YOU TRY!
'COURSE, I'D LOVE TO SEE YOU AS A CRATER.
SPACE RANGER
LIGHTYEAR

A little later...
ALL THIS PACKING MAKES ME HUNGRY. HOW 'BOUT DINNER AT, OH, PIZZA PLANET?
PIZZA PLANET! OH, BOY! CAN I BRING SOME TOYS?
YOU CAN BRING ONE TOY. NOW GO WASH YOUR HANDS.
TO INFINITY AND BEYOND!

When Andy left the room, Woody wondered whether he would get to go…

ONE TOY?

WILL ANDY PICK *ME?*

DON'T COUNT ON

The Magic 8 Ball gave its reply.

Disgusted, Woody dropped the ball. It rolled to the edge of the table and fell down a crack against the wall—

KLONK!

which gave him an idea.

BUZZ! OH, BUZZ LIGHTYEAR! WE'VE GOT TROUBLE!

TROUBLE? *WHERE?*

DOWN THERE. A HELPLESS TOY. IT'S *TRAPPED*, BUZZ!

THEN WE'VE GOT NO TIME TO LOSE!

WHERE IS IT? I DON'T SEE ANYTHING.
OH, HE'S THERE. JUST KEEP LOOKING.
When Buzz turned his back, Woody sent R.C. (Remote Control) racing straight toward him.
VROOM
WHAT KIND OF TOY— HEY!
CRASH
?!?
Buzz just got out of the way, but R.C. started a chain reaction…
that ended up with Buzz…

FALLING OUT THE WINDOW!!!
BUZZ!
BUZZ!
I DON'T SEE HIM. I THINK HE BOUNCED INTO SID'S YARD!

THIS WAS NO *ACCIDENT!* YOU BACKSTABBING *MURDERER!*
YOU—YOU DON'T THINK I *MEANT* TO THROW BUZZ OUT OF THE WINDOW, DO YOU?
IT WAS AN *ACCIDENT!* GUYS, C'MON NOW, YOU GOTTA *BELIEVE* ME!

WHERE IS YOUR HONOR, *DIRT-BAG?* YOU ARE AN ABSOLUTE *DISGRACE.*
MAGIC Etch A Sketch

THERE HE IS, MEN! *FRAG HIM!*

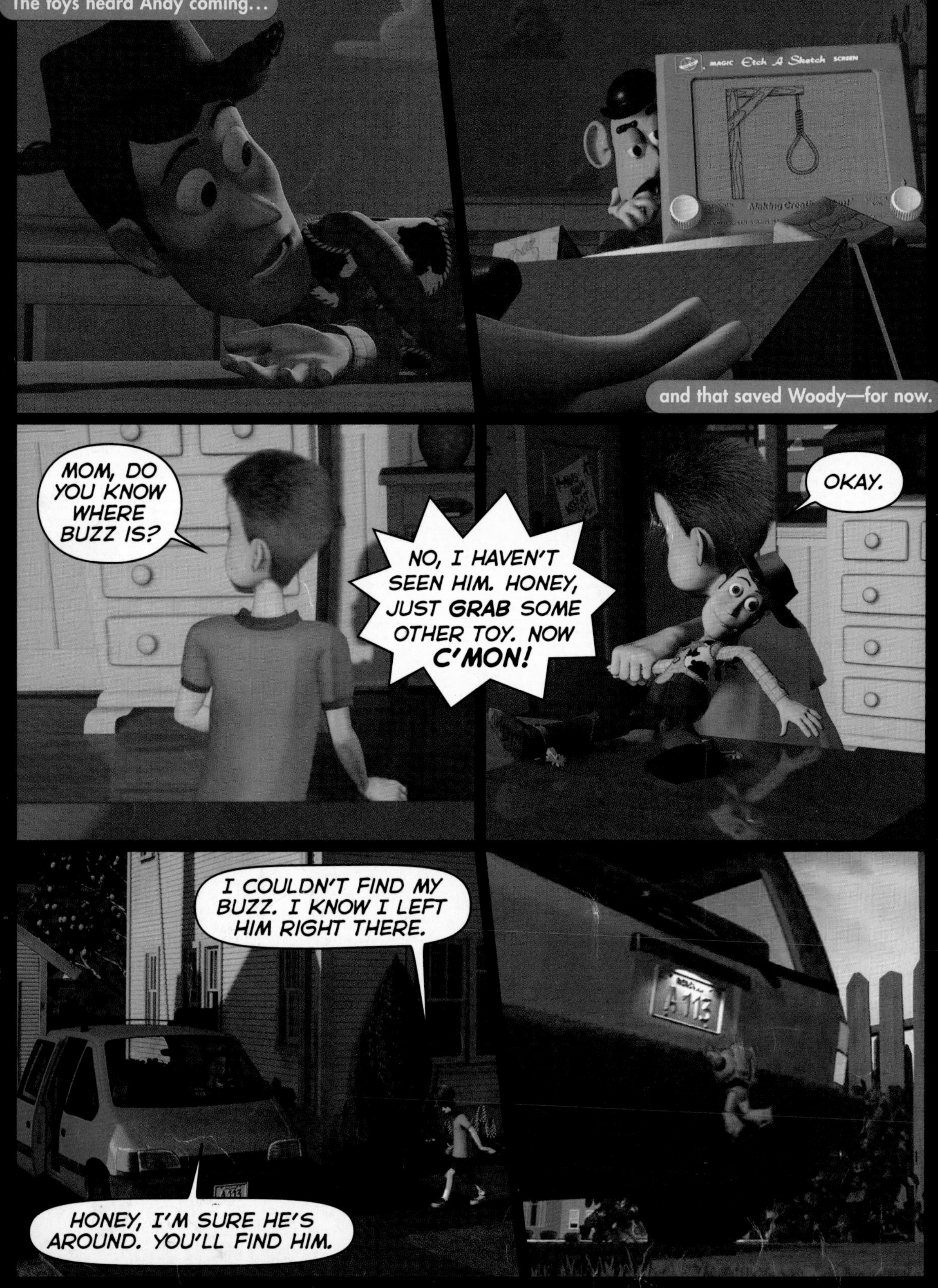
The toys heard Andy coming...
MAGIC Etch A Sketch SCREEN
and that saved Woody—for now.
MOM, DO YOU KNOW WHERE BUZZ IS?
NO, I HAVEN'T SEEN HIM. HONEY, JUST GRAB SOME OTHER TOY. NOW C'MON!
OKAY.
I COULDN'T FIND MY BUZZ. I KNOW I LEFT HIM RIGHT THERE.
HONEY, I'M SURE HE'S AROUND. YOU'LL FIND HIM.
A113

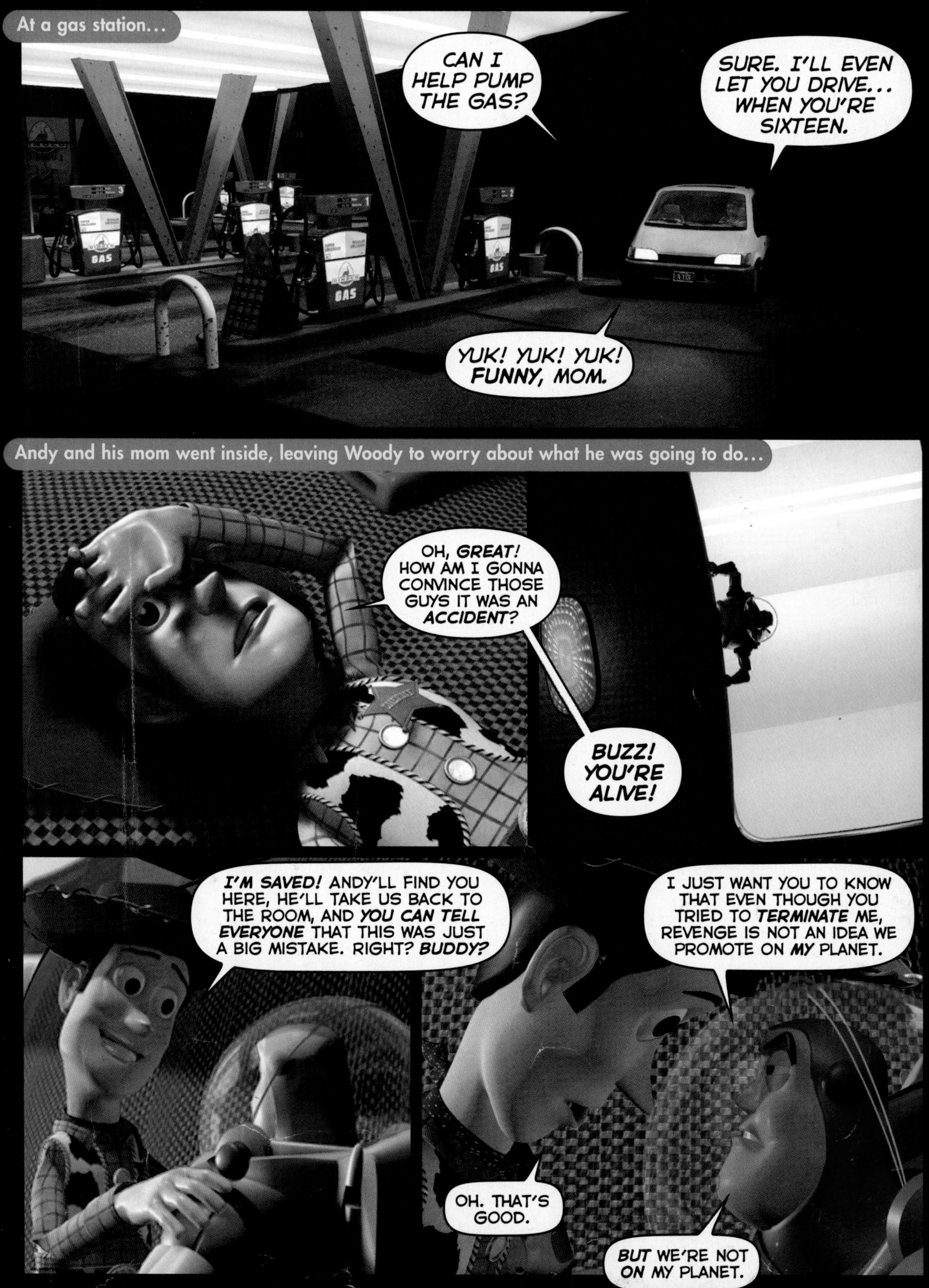

Andy and his mom went inside, leaving Woody to worry about what he was going to do...

OH, ***GREAT!*** HOW AM I GONNA CONVINCE THOSE GUYS IT WAS AN ***ACCIDENT?***

***BUZZ! YOU'RE ALIVE!***

***I'M SAVED!*** ANDY'LL FIND YOU HERE, HE'LL TAKE US BACK TO THE ROOM, AND ***YOU CAN TELL EVERYONE*** THAT THIS WAS JUST A BIG MISTAKE. RIGHT? ***BUDDY?***

I JUST WANT YOU TO KNOW THAT EVEN THOUGH YOU TRIED TO ***TERMINATE*** ME, REVENGE IS NOT AN IDEA WE PROMOTE ON ***MY*** PLANET.

OH. THAT'S GOOD.

***BUT*** WE'RE NOT ***ON*** MY PLANET.

Buzz and Woody fell out of the car and were too busy fighting to notice...

NEXT STOP...

PIZZA PLANET!
A 113
JET EXHAUST
Andy and his mom had returned. Off they drove!!!
SUPER UNLEADED
DINOCO
GAS
ANDY?! DOESN'T HE REALIZE THAT I'M NOT THERE?
I'M LOST! OH, I'M A LOST TOY!

SHERIFF, THIS IS NO TIME TO PANIC.
YOU IDIOT! THIS IS THE PERFECT TIME TO PANIC! I'M LOST, ANDY'S GONE, THEY'RE GOING TO MOVE FROM THEIR HOUSE IN TWO DAYS, AND IT'S ALL YOUR FAULT!
MY FAULT? IF YOU HADN'T PUSHED ME OUT OF THE WINDOW–

WHAT ARE YOU TALKING ABOUT?

OH, YEAH? IF YOU HADN'T TAKEN AWAY EVERYTHING THAT WAS IMPORTANT TO ME–
DON'T TALK TO ME ABOUT IMPORTANCE. BECAUSE OF YOU THE SECURITY OF THIS ENTIRE UNIVERSE IS IN JEOPARDY.

AND *YOU*, MY FRIEND, ARE RESPONSIBLE FOR *DELAYING* MY RENDEZVOUS WITH *STAR COMMAND.*

YOU ARE A TOY!

YOU AREN'T THE REAL BUZZ LIGHTYEAR! YOU'RE A SMALL ACTION FIGURE! YOU ARE A CHILD'S PLAYTHING!

Buzz had no idea what Woody was talking about, and he decided to head out on his own.

Just then a truck pulled into the station.

HEY, GAS, DUDE!

PIZZA PLANET?!? *ANDY!*

OH, NO! I CAN'T SHOW MY FACE IN THAT ROOM WITHOUT *BUZZ!*

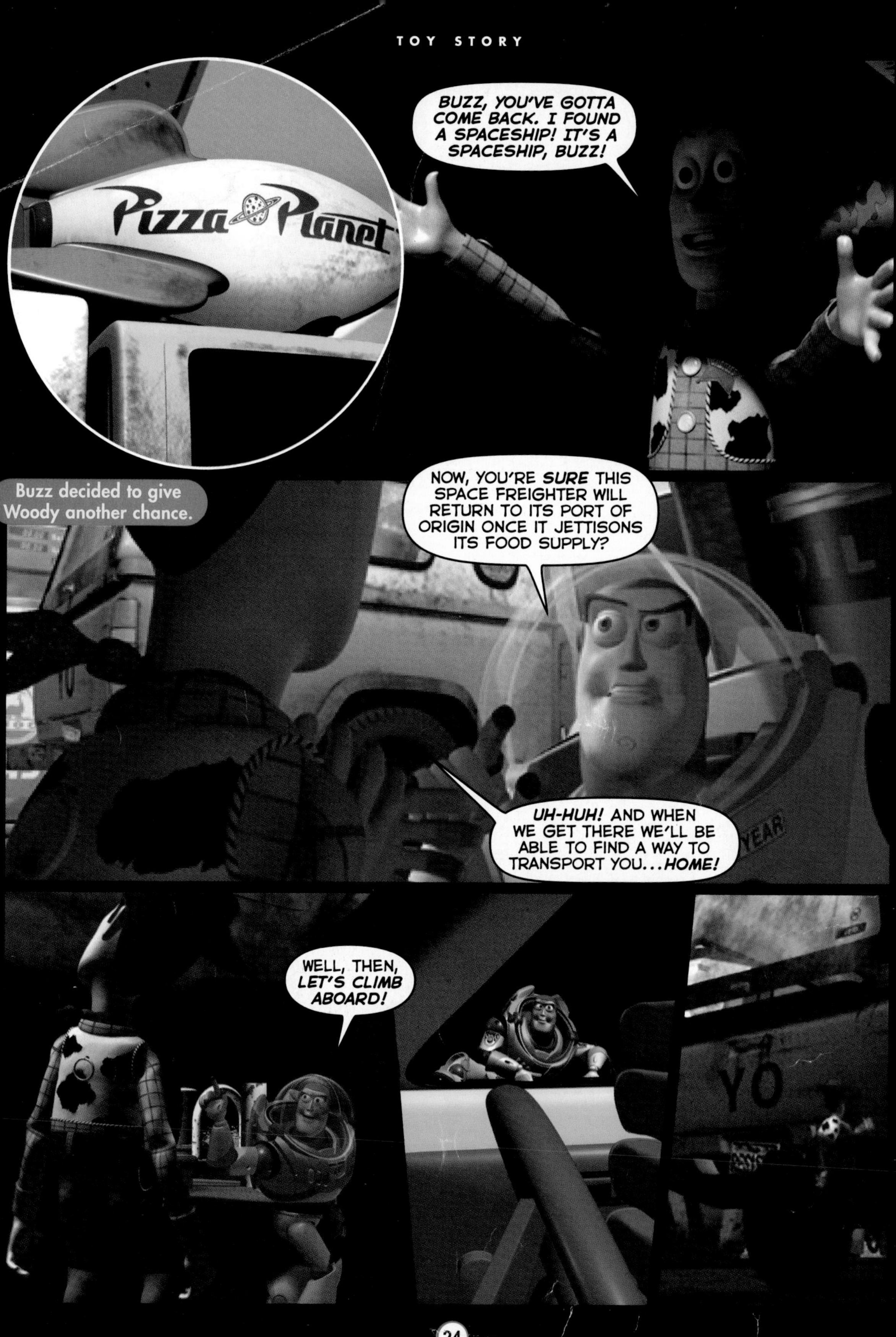
Pizza Planet
BUZZ, YOU'VE GOTTA COME BACK. I FOUND A SPACESHIP! IT'S A SPACESHIP, BUZZ!
Buzz decided to give Woody another chance.
NOW, YOU'RE *SURE* THIS SPACE FREIGHTER WILL RETURN TO ITS PORT OF ORIGIN ONCE IT JETTISONS ITS FOOD SUPPLY?
*UH-HUH!* AND WHEN WE GET THERE WE'LL BE ABLE TO FIND A WAY TO TRANSPORT YOU...*HOME!*
WELL, THEN, *LET'S CLIMB ABOARD!*

Buzz couldn't believe it!

Inside, Woody searched desperately.
?!?
ANDY!
BUZZ, WHEN I SAY "GO," WE'RE GONNA JUMP IN THE BASKET.
But when Woody turned around, he found Buzz had run off…
THIS CANNOT BE HAPPENING TO ME!
CRANE
PRIZE
to a nearby spaceship…
GREETINGS! I AM BUZZ LIGHTYEAR! I COME IN PEACE!
THIS IS AN INTERGALACTIC EMERGENCY! I NEED TO COMMANDEER YOUR VESSEL TO SECTOR 12.
WHO'S IN CHARGE HERE?
A STRANGER!
FROM THE OUTSIDE!
where Buzz met the natives.

THE CLA-A-A-A-A-A-A-W!

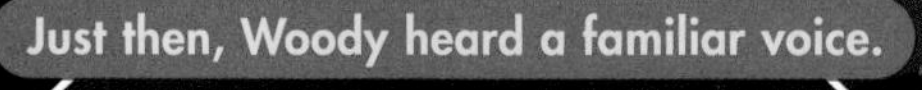
Just then, Woody heard a familiar voice.
HA HA HA HA!
OH, NO! SID!
THE CLAW IS OUR MASTER! THE CLAW CHOOSES WHO WILL GO AND WHO WILL STAY!
GET DOWN!
SH-H-H-H. THE CLA-A-A-A-A-A-W!
WHAT'S GOTTEN INTO YOU, SHERIFF?
YOU ARE THE ONE WHO DECIDED TO CLIMB INTO THIS !
IT MO-O-O-O-VES!

From high above, the claw descended.
I HAVE BEEN CHOSEN!
Then Sid spotted an even bigger prize!
A BUZZ LIGHTYEAR! NO WAY!
YES!
CLINK!
BUZZ, NO!
HE MUST GO-O-O-O!
DO NOT FIGHT THE CLA-A-A-A-AW!
NEXT LAUNCH:
ALL RIGHT! DOUBLE PRIZES!
LET'S GO HOME AND PLAY! HA-HA-HA.
Meanwhile, Andy had returned from Pizza Planet.
MOM, HAVE YOU SEEN WOODY? WOODY'S GONE!

Little did Andy know Woody and Buzz were inside Sid's backpack and heading to the house next door.
SHERIFF! I CAN SEE YOUR DWELLING FROM HERE! YOU'RE ALMOST *HOME.*
YOU GUYS DON'T *GET IT*, DO YOU? ONCE WE GO INTO SID'S HOUSE, WE *WON'T* BE COMING OUT.
NIRVANA IS COMING! THE MYSTIC PORTAL AWAITS!
GRRRR
LOOK! JANIE'S SICK!
NO, SHE'S NOT! DON'T TOUCH HER!
Buzz and Woody watched in horror as Sid tossed the little alien to his dog, Scud, and then grabbed his sister's favorite doll, Janie.

Up the stairs they went, straight into Sid's den of doom.
WE HAVE A SICK PATIENT HERE, NURSE. PREPARE THE O.R.!
I'LL HAVE TO PERFORM ONE OF MY... OPERATIONS!
NO ONE'S EVER ATTEMPTED A DOUBLE BYPASS BRAIN TRANSPLANT BEFORE.
OH, NO!
I DON'T BELIEVE THAT MAN'S EVER BEEN TO MEDICAL SCHOOL.
NOW FOR THE TRICKY PART- PLIERS!
JANIE'S ALL BETTER NOW.
NOOOO! MOM! MOM!
WE'RE GONNA DIE.

Sid finally left his room. All was dark...but not silent.

SCRITCH

SCREE!

UH, BUZZ, WAS THAT Y-Y-YOU?

CLIK!

CLIK!

*HEY!* HI THERE, LITTLE FELLA! DO YOU KNOW A WAY OUT OF HERE?

CLIK!

CLIK!

YAAAAAH!

B-B-B-BUZZ!

From all corners of the room, strange creatures emerged...

Mutant toys cobbled together by Sid in his workshop of terror! Thinking they were cannibals, Woody fought his way past them using Buzz's karate-chop arm.



As Woody tiptoed away, his pull string caught on the railing.

YEE-HAW! GIDDYAP, PARDNER!
BLINK!
BLINK!

Buzz and Woody decided to split up and hide.

WHEW!
From behind him Buzz suddenly heard a voice—
CALLING BUZZ LIGHTYEAR! THIS IS STAR COMMAND. BUZZ LIGHTYEAR! DO YOU READ ME?

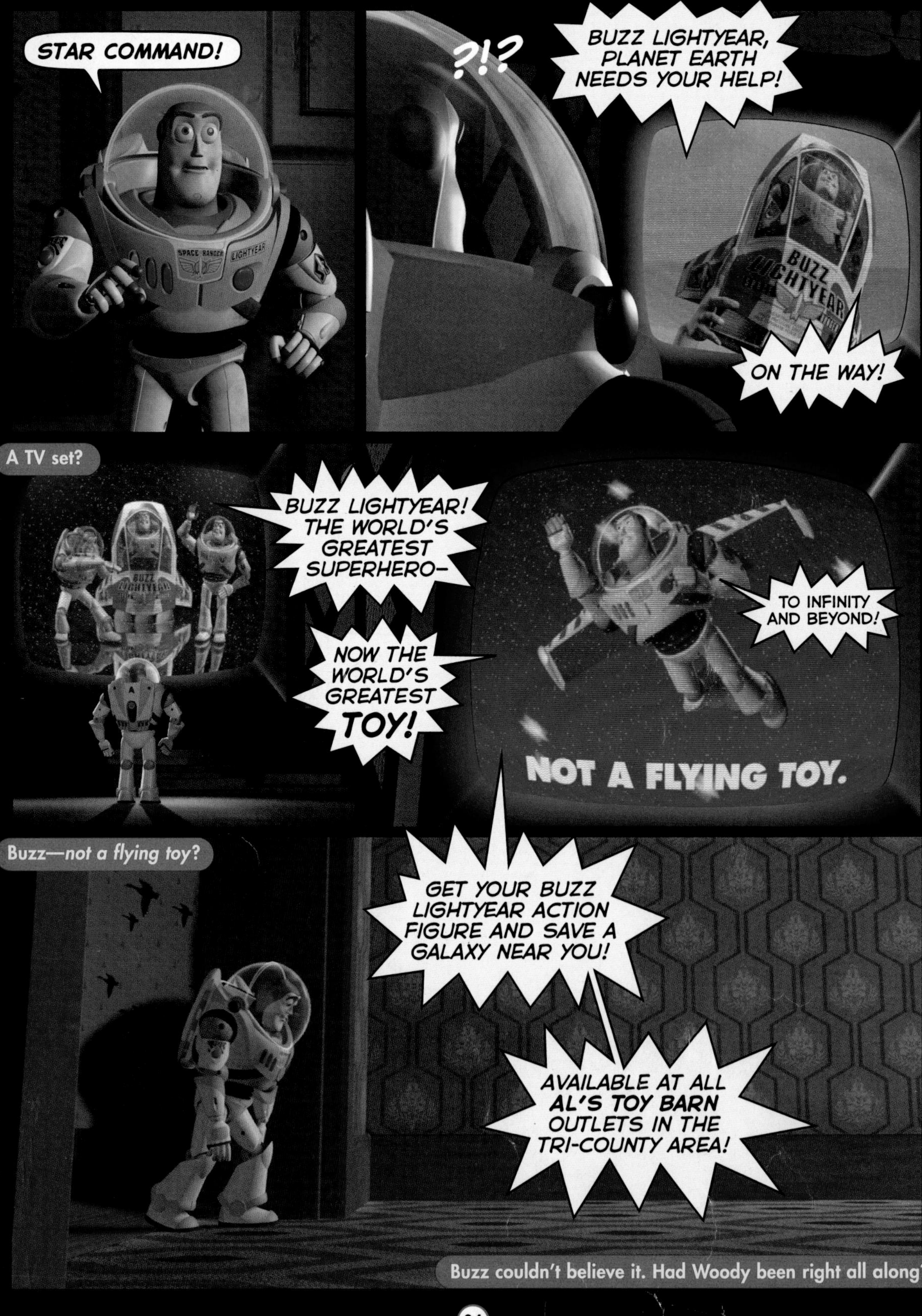
STAR COMMAND!
?!?
BUZZ LIGHTYEAR, PLANET EARTH NEEDS YOUR HELP!
ON THE WAY!
A TV set?
BUZZ LIGHTYEAR! THE WORLD'S GREATEST SUPERHERO—
NOW THE WORLD'S GREATEST TOY!
TO INFINITY AND BEYOND!
NOT A FLYING TOY.
Buzz—*not a flying toy?*
GET YOUR BUZZ LIGHTYEAR ACTION FIGURE AND SAVE A GALAXY NEAR YOU!
AVAILABLE AT ALL AL'S TOY BARN OUTLETS IN THE TRI-COUNTY AREA!
Buzz couldn't believe it. Had Woody been right all along?

Buzz decided to find out—once and for all!

TO INFINITY...
AND...

BEYOOOOOND!
LIGHTYEAR
ANDY

MOM? HAVE YOU SEEN MY DOLL?

NEVER MIND.

When Woody finally found him, Buzz had lost an arm and was dressed for a tea party.
WHAT HAPPENED TO *YOU?*
ONE MINUTE YOU'RE DEFENDING THE *WHOLE* GALAXY, AND *SUDDENLY* YOU FIND YOURSELF *SUCKING DOWN DARJEELING.*
SPACE RANGER LIGHTYEAR
I THINK YOU'VE HAD ENOUGH *TEA* FOR TODAY. LET'S GET YOU OUT OF HERE, BUZZ.
*AH-HA! AH-HA!*
*SNAP OUT OF IT, BUZZ!*
SORRY. I'M JUST A LITTLE *DEPRESSED.*
OH, I'M A *SHAM!* I CAN'T EVEN FLY OUT A *WINDOW!*
YEARS OF ACADEMY TRAINING—*WASTED!*
OUT THE *WINDOW!* BUZZ, YOU'RE A *GENIUS!*
From Sid's window, Woody could see Andy's room!
*HEY, GUYS! GUYS! HEY!*

WOODY?
SON OF A BUILDING BLOCK, IT'S WOODY!
YOU'RE KIDDING!
HE'S IN THE PSYCHO'S BEDROOM!
BOY, AM I GLAD TO SEE YOU GUYS. HERE, CATCH THIS.
NOW JUST TIE IT ON TO SOMETHING.
DID YOU ALL TAKE STUPID PILLS THIS MORNING? HAVE YOU FORGOTTEN WHAT HE DID TO BUZZ?
AND NOW YOU WANT TO LET HIM BACK OVER HERE?

YOU GOT IT ALL WRONG, POTATO HEAD. BUZZ IS FINE! BUZZ IS RIGHT HERE. HE'S WITH ME!
YOU ARE A LIAR!
BUZZ, WILL YOU GET UP HERE AND GIVE ME A HAND?
LA-DI-DA-DI-DA.
VERY FUNNY. BUZZ! THIS IS SERIOUS!
KLUNK!
Desperate to escape, Woody tried one last gambit.
OH, HI, BUZZ! WHY DON'T YOU SAY "HELLO" TO THE GUYS OVER THERE?
"HI YA, FELLAS. TO INFINITY AND BEYOND!"
YEAH, HEY, BUZZ. LET'S SH THE GUYS OUR SECRET BEST FRIENDS HAND SHAKE. GIMME FIVE, MAN!

Suddenly there were footsteps outside the door. Everyone hid—except Buzz.
UH, S THO YOU W YOU MY
SO YOU SEE? WE'RE FRIENDS NOW, GUYS. AREN'T WE, BUZZ?
OOPS!
FAT COW FARMS
I HOPE SID PULELY YOUR VOICEBOUS. OUT, YA CREE OF OF N."
YOU MURDERING DOG!
OH, THAT IS DISGUSTING.
SO...WHAT AM I GONNA BLOW?
AAAAW!
Buzz, it started raining, so Sid d the launch until the morning.

During the night, Woody pleaded with Buzz...
PSST! BUZZ! GET THIS TOOLBOX OFF ME. I NEED YOUR HELP.
I CAN'T HELP ANYONE.
SURE YOU CAN. YOU GET ME OUT OF HERE, AND I'LL GET THAT ROCKET OFF YOU, AND WE'LL MAKE A BREAK FOR ANDY'S HOUSE.
ANDY'S HOUSE. SID'S HOUSE. WHAT'S THE DIFFERENCE?
YOU HAD A BIG FALL. YOU MUST NOT BE THINKING CLEARLY.
NO, FOR THE FIRST TIME, I AM THINKING CLEARLY. YOU WERE RIGHT. I'M NOT A SPACE RANGER. I'M JUST A TOY.
WHOA! BEING A TOY IS A LOT BETTER. ANDY THINKS YOU'RE THE GREATEST, AND NOT BECAUSE YOU'RE A SPACE RANGER, PAL. BECAUSE YOU'RE A TOY. HIS TOY.
WHY WOULD ANDY WANT ME?
LOOK AT YOU! YOU'RE A BUZZ LIGHTYEAR! YOU ARE A COOL TOY.
IN FACT, YOU'RE TOO COOL. WHAT CHANCE DOES A TOY LIKE ME HAVE AGAINST A BUZZ LIGHTYEAR? WHY WOULD ANDY PLAY WITH ME WHEN HE'S GOT YOU?

I'M THE ONE WHO SHOULD BE STRAPPED TO THAT ROCKET.

LISTEN, BUZZ. *FORGET* ABOUT ME. YOU SHOULD GET OUT OF HERE WHILE YOU CAN.

Dawn arrived...

BUZZ, WHAT ARE YOU DOING?

SHERIFF, THERE'S A KID OVER IN THAT HOUSE WHO *NEEDS* US. NOW LET'S GET YOU OUT OF THIS THING.

WOODY! I HEAR THE MOVING VAN!

WE'VE GOT TO GET OUT OF HERE—*NOW!*

Buzz pushed...

ALMOST—UNHHH!

THERE—UNHHHHH!

and pushed!!!

Suddenly the alarm went off and Sid woke up.



He grabbed Buzz and headed outside.



Woody had only one hope left...

The mutant toys gathered around Woody...



who explained his plan.

Legs and Ducky got into position.

Legs dropped Ducky down in front of the door.

And Ducky gave the signal!

DING DONG!

AARPH

Scud rushed outside—just as Ducky vanished.

GO!

Woody and crew flew down the stairs...

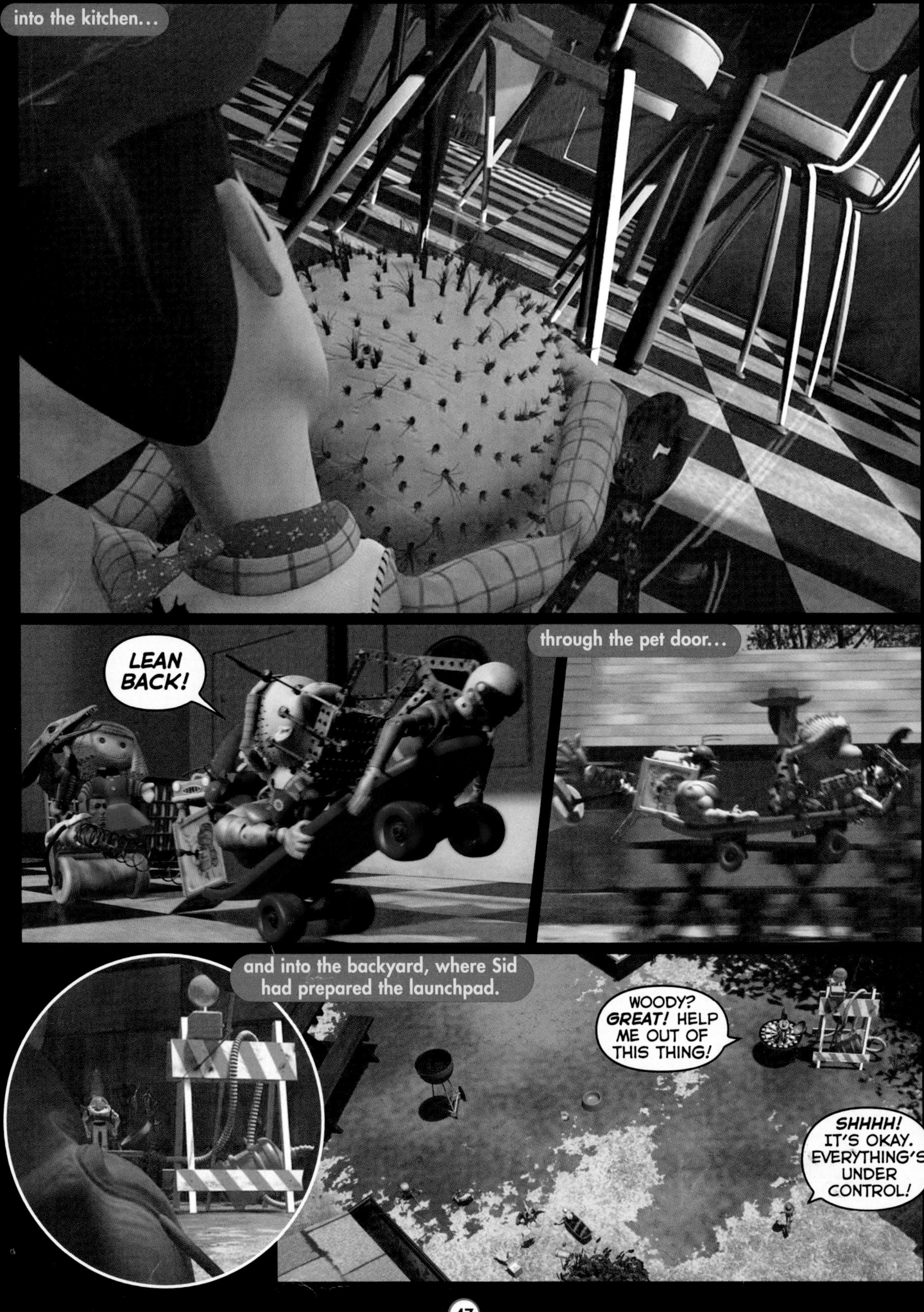

into the kitchen...

As Sid emerged from his control room, Woody flopped down on the ground.
HOUSTON, ALL SYSTEMS ARE GO. REQUESTING PERMISSION TO LAUNCH.
HEY! HOW'D YOU GET HERE?
Sid put a match in Woody's pocket and flung him on the grill.
OH, WELL. YOU AND I CAN HAVE A COOKOUT LATER. HA! HA!
TEN! NINE! EIGHT! SEVEN! SIX! FIVE! FOUR! THREE! TWO! ONE–
REACH FOR THE SKY!
HUH?

THIS TOWN AIN'T BIG
ENOUGH FOR THE TWO OF US!

*WHAT?*

SOMEBODY POISONED
THE WATER HOLE!

*IT'S BUSTED!*

WHO ARE YOU CALLING
BUSTED, BUSTER?

**Woody had given his signal!
The mutant toys attacked!**

*YAAAAAAH!*

THAT'S RIGHT! I'M TALKING
TO YOU, SID PHILLIPS.

WE DON'T LIKE BEING
BLOWN UP, SID. OR
SMASHED, OR RIPPED APART!

*W-W-W-WE?*

THAT'S RIGHT. YOUR TOYS.

FROM NOW ON, SID, YOU MUST TAKE GOOD CARE OF YOUR TOYS. BECAUSE IF YOU DON'T, WE'LL FIND OUT, SID.
SO PLAY NICE.
WE TOYS CAN SEE EVERYTHING!
AAAAAAGGGHHH!!!
NICE WORK, FELLAS!
YA-HOOOOOO!

Woody had saved the day...
WOODY! THANKS.
VROOM
WE GOTTA RUN!
but there was still a car to catch!
A 113
KLONK!
Just when Woody thought they had made it, Buzz got stuck.
C'MON, BUZZ. LET'S GO!
Andy's car was gone...

but not the moving van!
EGGMAN MOVERS
Moving the most Coast to Coast.™
YOU CAN DO IT, WOODY!
WHEW! I MADE IT!
HOLD ON, WOODY!
AAAAAH! GET AWAY, YOU STUPID DOG! DOWN! DOWN!
I CAN'T DO IT! TAKE CARE OF ANDY FOR ME!

Buzz came to Woody's rescue.

Scud shook Buzz off and chased him under a car.

WHERE ARE YOU, R.C.? WHERE?
WHAT? ARE WE THERE ALREADY?
WOODY?! HOW'D YOU–
AHA! THERE YOU ARE!
HEY! WHAT'S HE DOING?
HE'S AT IT AGAIN!
Woody tossed R.C. out of the truck and sent him after Buzz—this time to save him!
HURRY, BUZZ, GET ON!

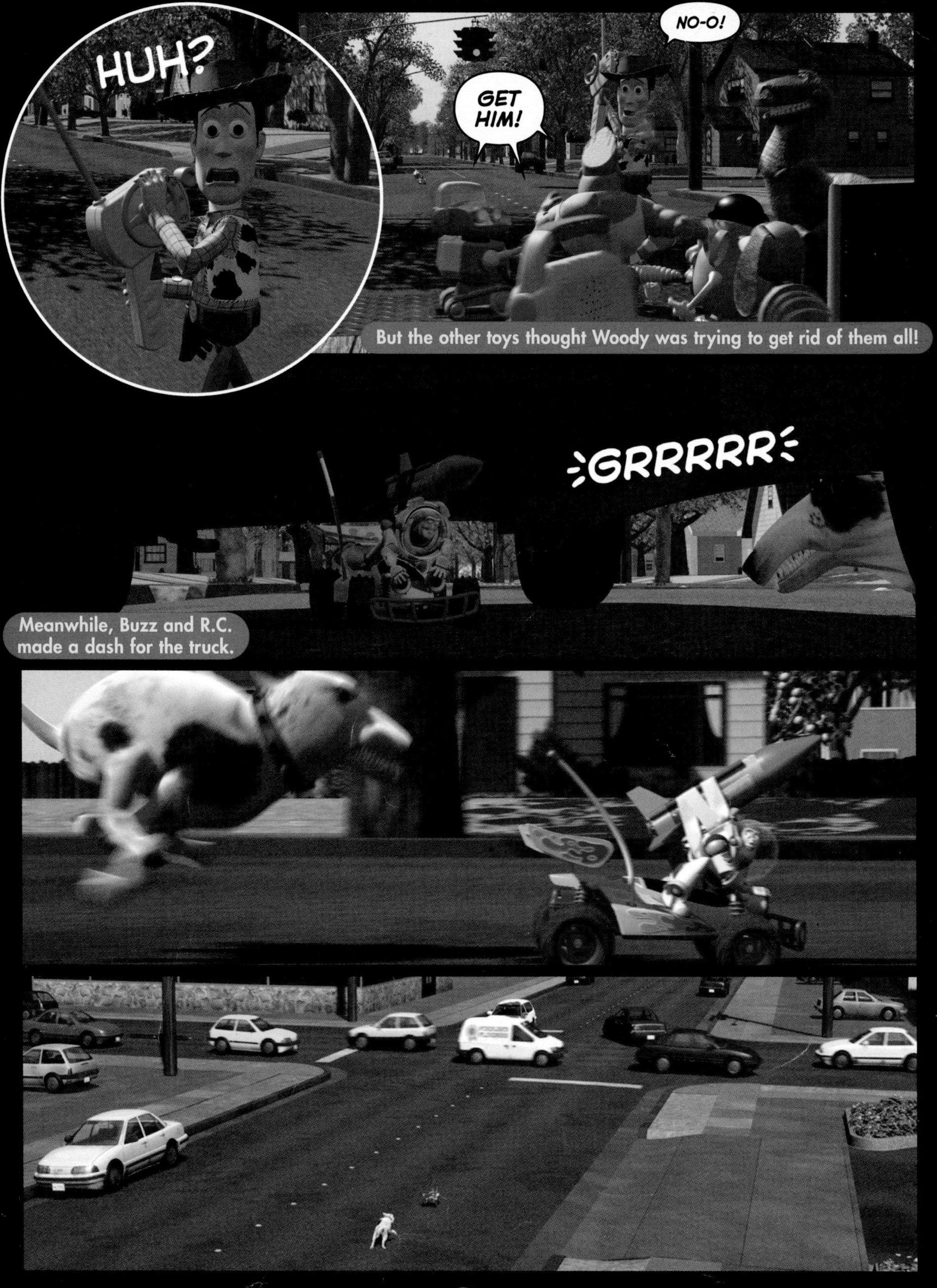

But the other toys thought Woody was trying to get rid of them all!

GRRRRR

Meanwhile, Buzz and R.C. made a dash for the truck.

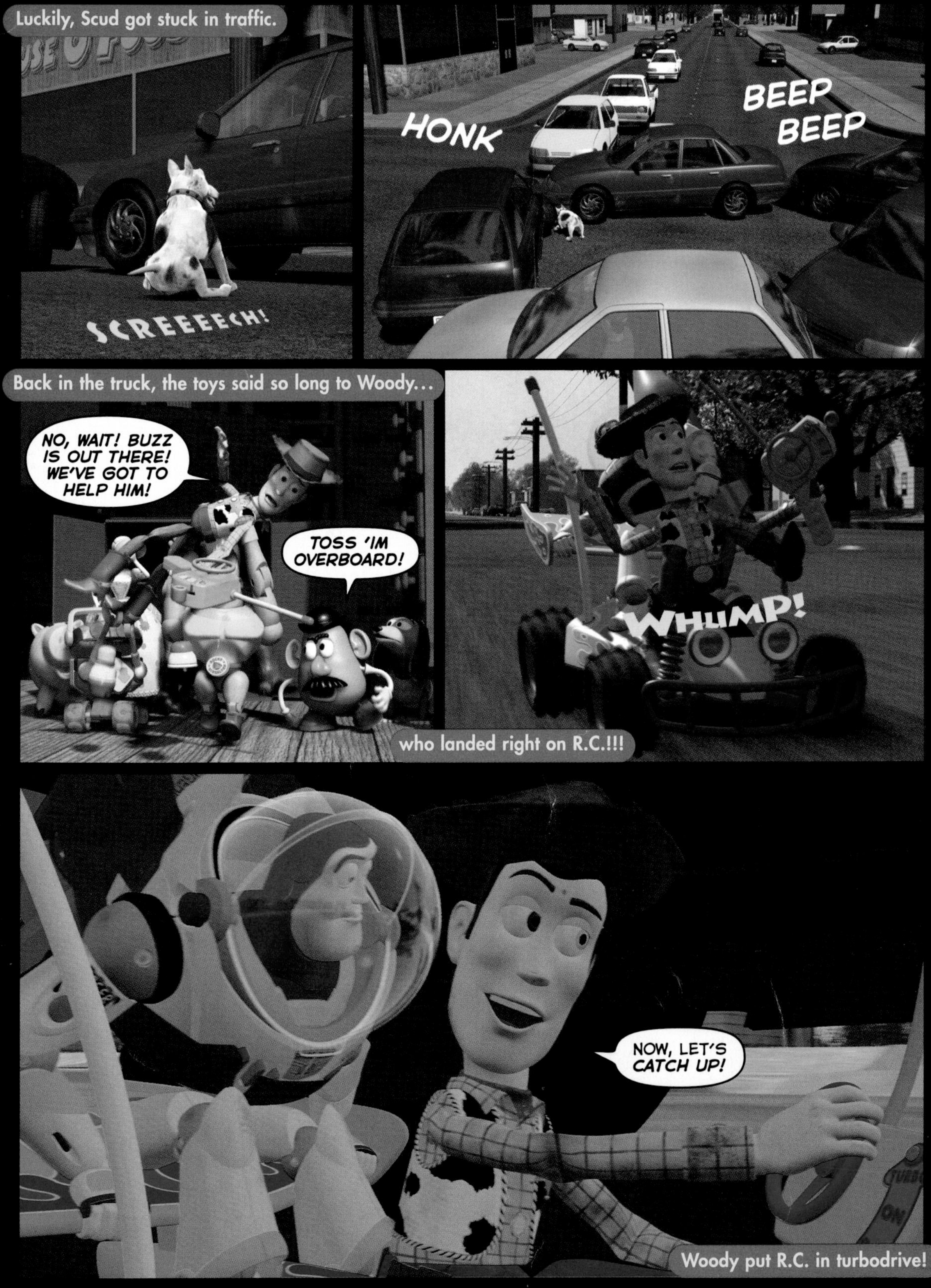

Luckily, Scud got stuck in traffic.

Back in the truck, the toys said so long to Woody...

who landed right on R.C.!!!

NOW, LET'S CATCH UP!

Woody put R.C. in turbodrive!

GUYS! WOODY'S RIDING R.C.! AND BUZZ IS WITH HIM!

WHAT???

IT IS BUZZ! WOODY WAS TELLING THE TRUTH!

LOWER THE RAMP!

WE'RE ALMOST THERE!

WOODY! SPEED UP!

THE BATTERIES! THEY'RE RUNNING OUT!

SLINK! HANG ON!

R-R-R-R-R-R

Then they remembered—
WOODY! THE ROCKET!
THE MATCH!
YES! THANK YOU, SID!
But a car sped by and out went the match.
POOF!
NO!
NO! NO! NO! NO! NO-O-O-O-O-O-O!
?!?
Woody thought it was all over...

And then he noticed a burning spot on his hand...
BUZZ?
coming from the sun...
WOODY, WHAT ARE YOU DOING?
HOLD STILL, BUZZ.
shining through Buzz's helmet!!!
HA HA!
YOU DID IT! NEXT STOP, ANDY!
WAIT A MINUTE! I JUST LIT A ROCKET...
SSSSSSSSSSSSSSS

AND...
ROCKETS...
EXPLODE!

AGGHHH!! THIS IS THE PART WHERE WE BLOW UP!

POP!
POP!

POW!

NOT TODAY!
AHH!!

BUZZ?!? YOU'RE FLYING!

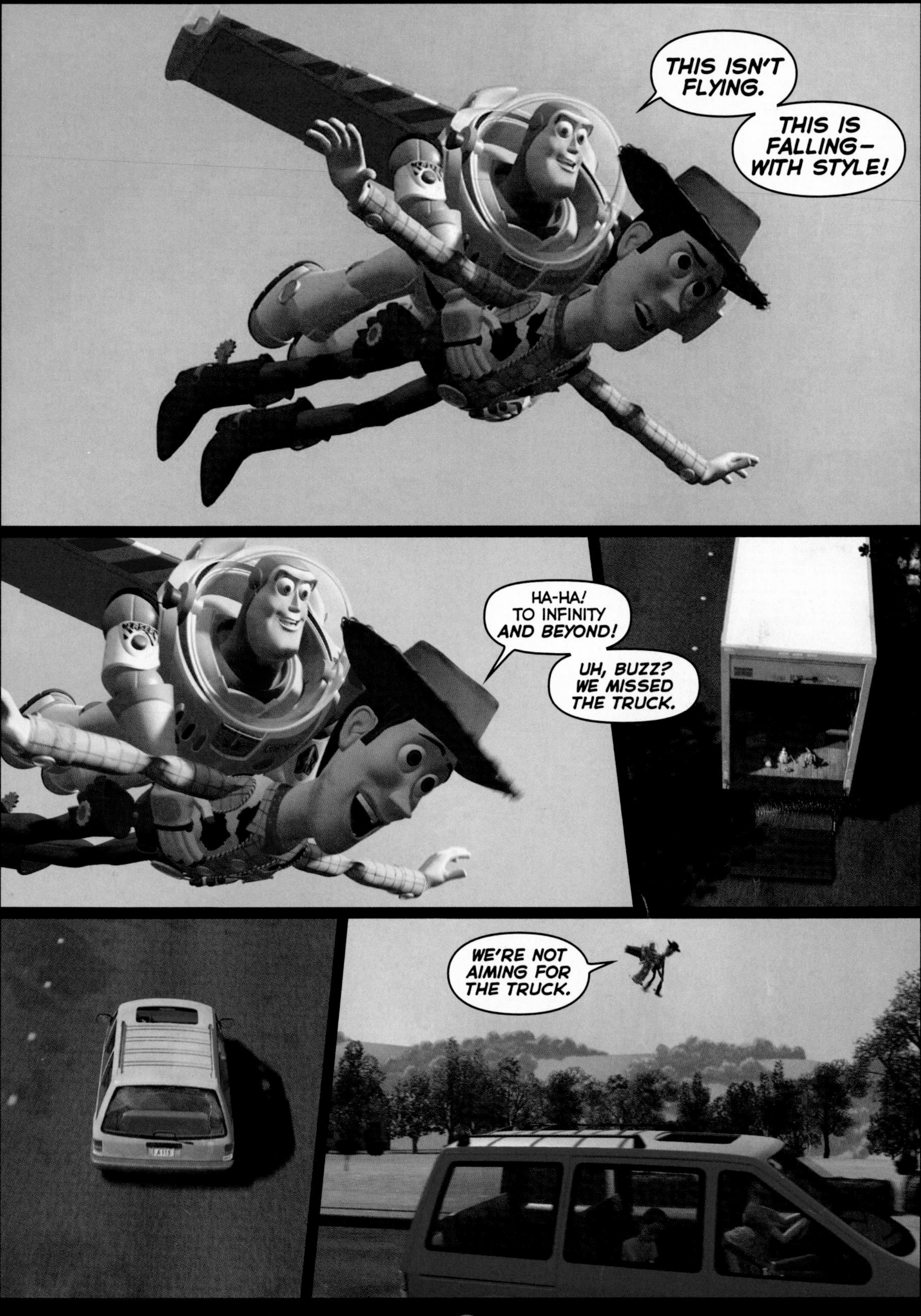

THIS ISN'T FLYING.
THIS IS FALLING—WITH STYLE!

Buzz and Woody didn't say a word.

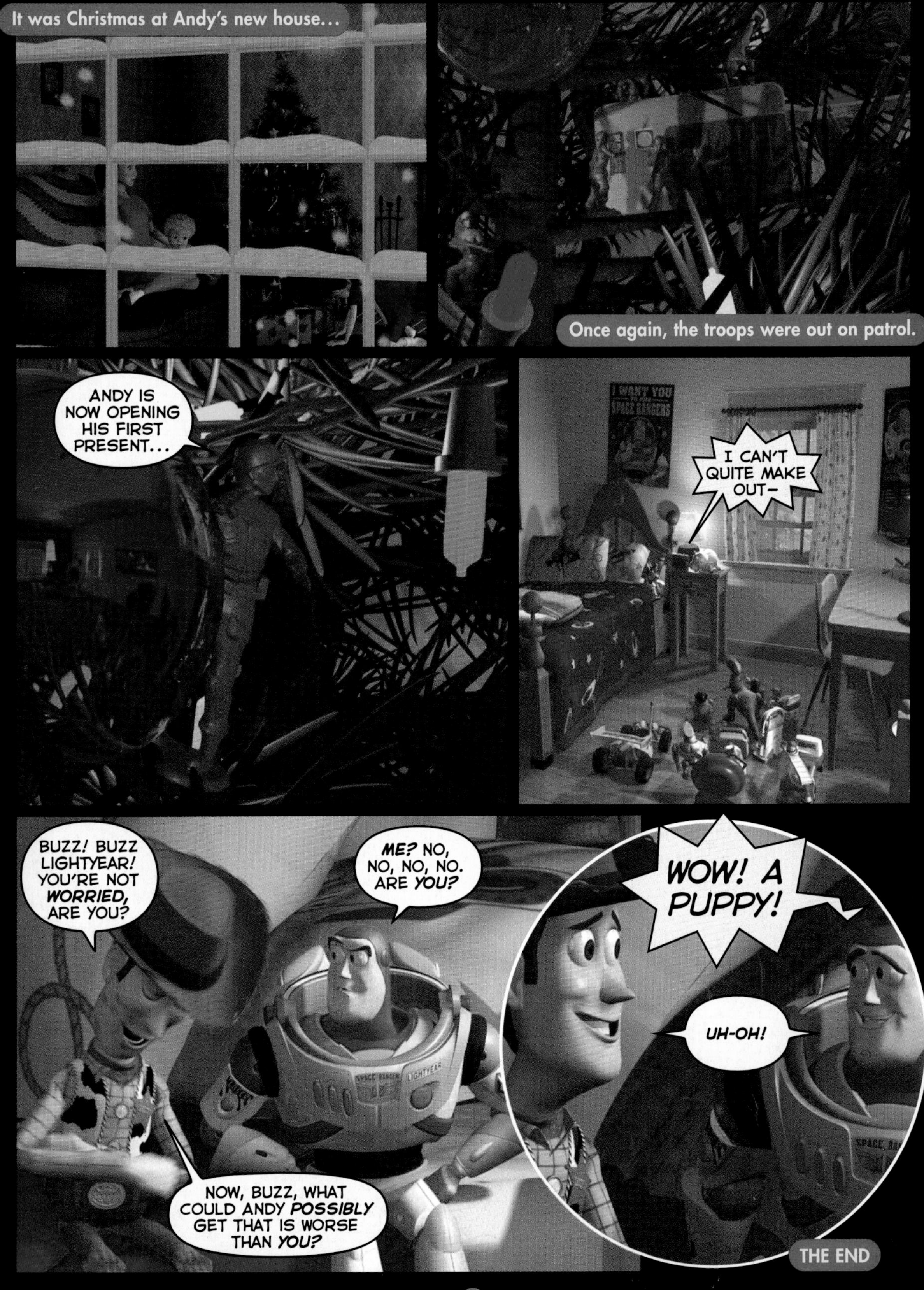

It was Christmas at Andy's new house...
Once again, the troops were out on patrol.
ANDY IS NOW OPENING HIS FIRST PRESENT...
I CAN'T QUITE MAKE OUT–
BUZZ! BUZZ LIGHTYEAR! YOU'RE NOT *WORRIED*, ARE YOU?
*ME?* NO, NO, NO, NO. ARE *YOU?*
NOW, BUZZ, WHAT COULD ANDY *POSSIBLY* GET THAT IS WORSE THAN *YOU?*
WOW! A PUPPY!
UH-OH!
THE END

Disney · PIXAR

TOY STORY 2

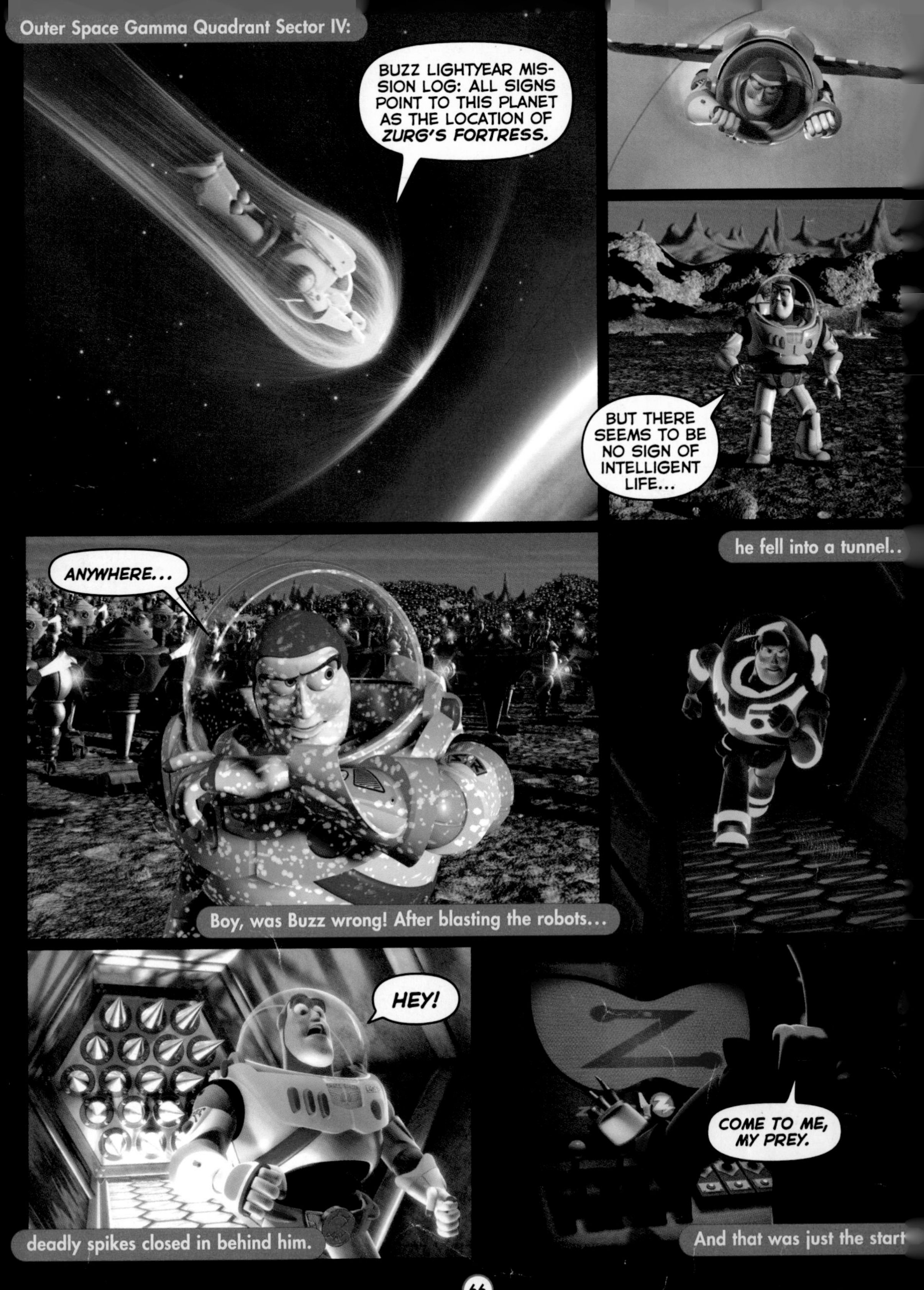

Outer Space Gamma Quadrant Sector IV:

BUZZ LIGHTYEAR MISSION LOG: ALL SIGNS POINT TO THIS PLANET AS THE LOCATION OF *ZURG'S FORTRESS.*

BUT THERE SEEMS TO BE NO SIGN OF INTELLIGENT LIFE...

Boy, was Buzz wrong! After blasting the robots...

he fell into a tunnel..

deadly spikes closed in behind him.

And that was just the start

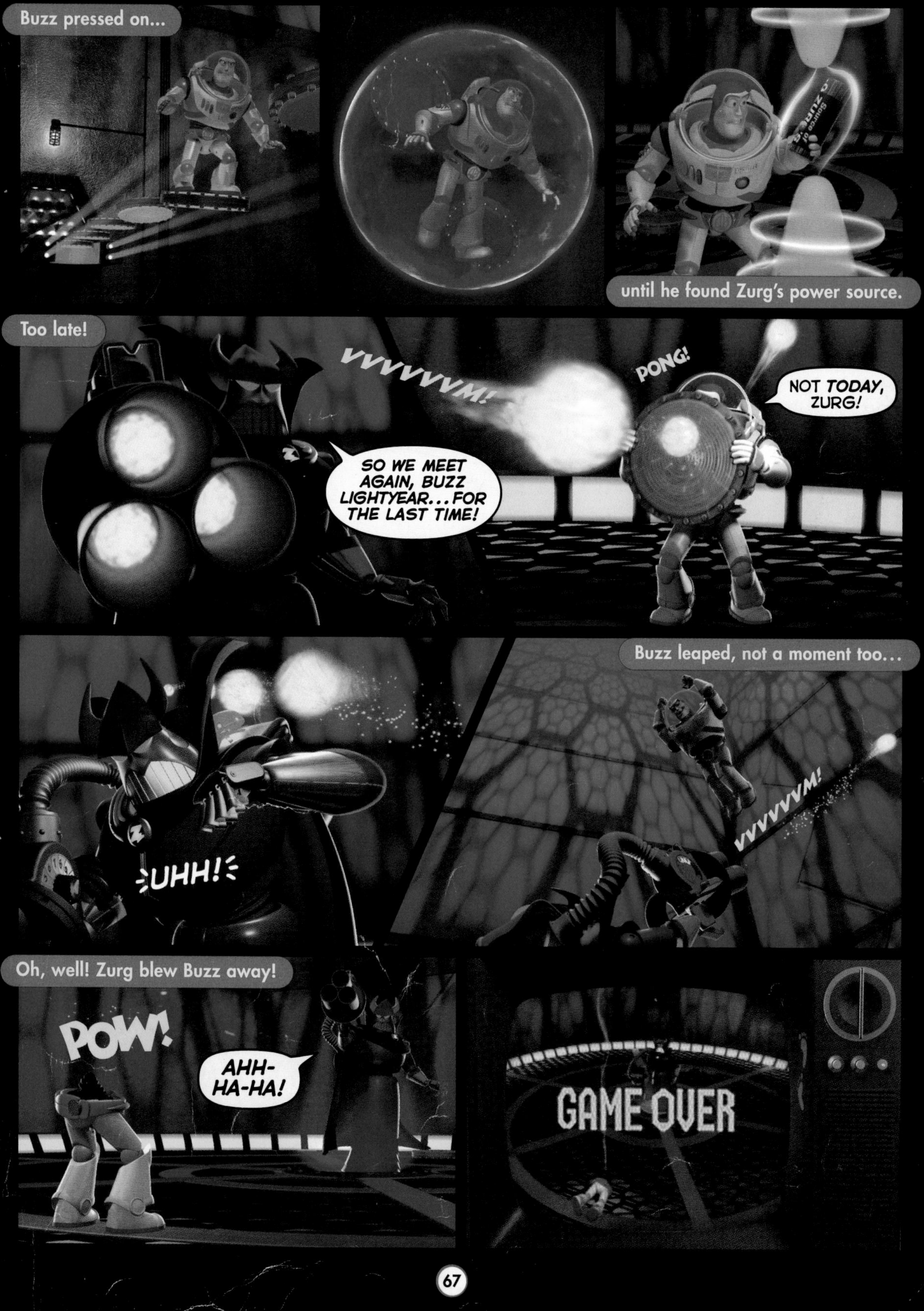

Buzz pressed on...

until he found Zurg's power source.

Too late!

VVVVVVVM!

SO WE MEET AGAIN, BUZZ LIGHTYEAR...FOR THE LAST TIME!

PONG!

NOT *TODAY,* ZURG!

UHH!

Buzz leaped, not a moment too...

VVVVVVM!

Oh, well! Zurg blew Buzz away!

POW!

AHH-HA-HA!

GAME OVER

NO!!!
NO, NO, NO,
NO, NO!
OH! YOU ALMOST HAD HIM!
I'M NEVER GONNA DEFEAT ZURG!
SURE YOU WILL, REX. IN FACT, YOU'RE A BETTER BUZZ THAN I AM.
Buzz wanted to help Rex defeat Zurg...
but right now another toy needed him.
ZOOOP!
WHERE IS IT? OH, WHERE IS IT, WHERE IS IT?
OKAY, BUZZ. HERE'S THE LIST OF THINGS TO DO WHILE I'M GONE: BATTERIES CHANGED, TOYS ROTATED...
YOU HAVEN'T FOUND YOUR HAT, HAVE YOU?
NO! ANDY'S LEAVING FOR COWBOY CAMP AND I CAN'T FIND IT ANYWHERE!
PLUNK!
RIGHT!
HAS ANYBODY FOUND WOODY'S HAT?

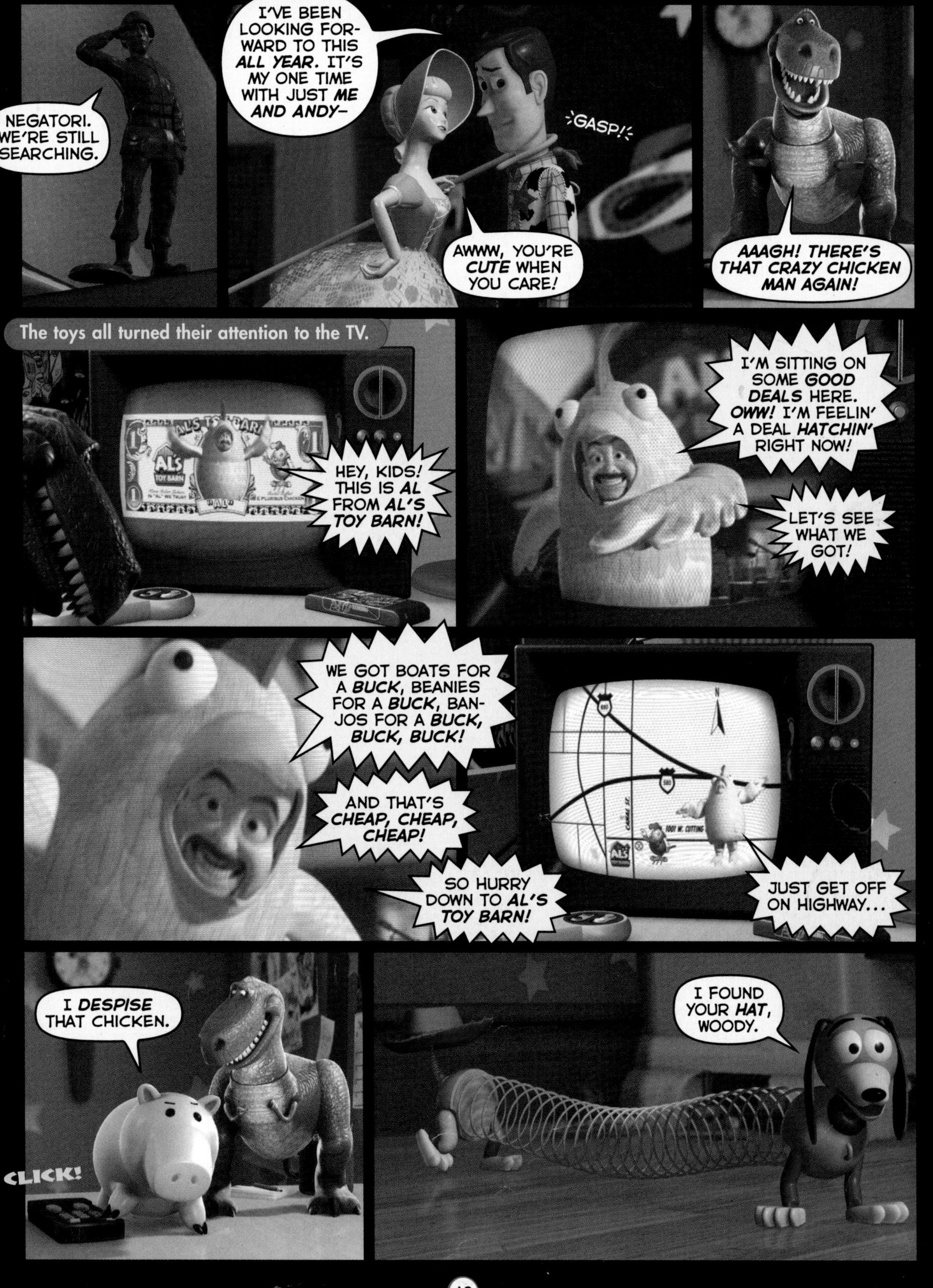

NEGATORI. WE'RE STILL SEARCHING.

I'VE BEEN LOOKING FORWARD TO THIS *ALL YEAR*. IT'S MY ONE TIME WITH JUST *ME AND ANDY*—

GASP!

AWWW, YOU'RE *CUTE* WHEN YOU CARE!

*AAAGH! THERE'S THAT CRAZY CHICKEN MAN AGAIN!*

The toys all turned their attention to the TV.

HEY, KIDS! THIS IS *AL* FROM *AL'S TOY BARN!*

I'M SITTING ON SOME *GOOD DEALS* HERE. *OWW!* I'M FEELIN' A DEAL *HATCHIN'* RIGHT NOW!

LET'S SEE WHAT WE GOT!

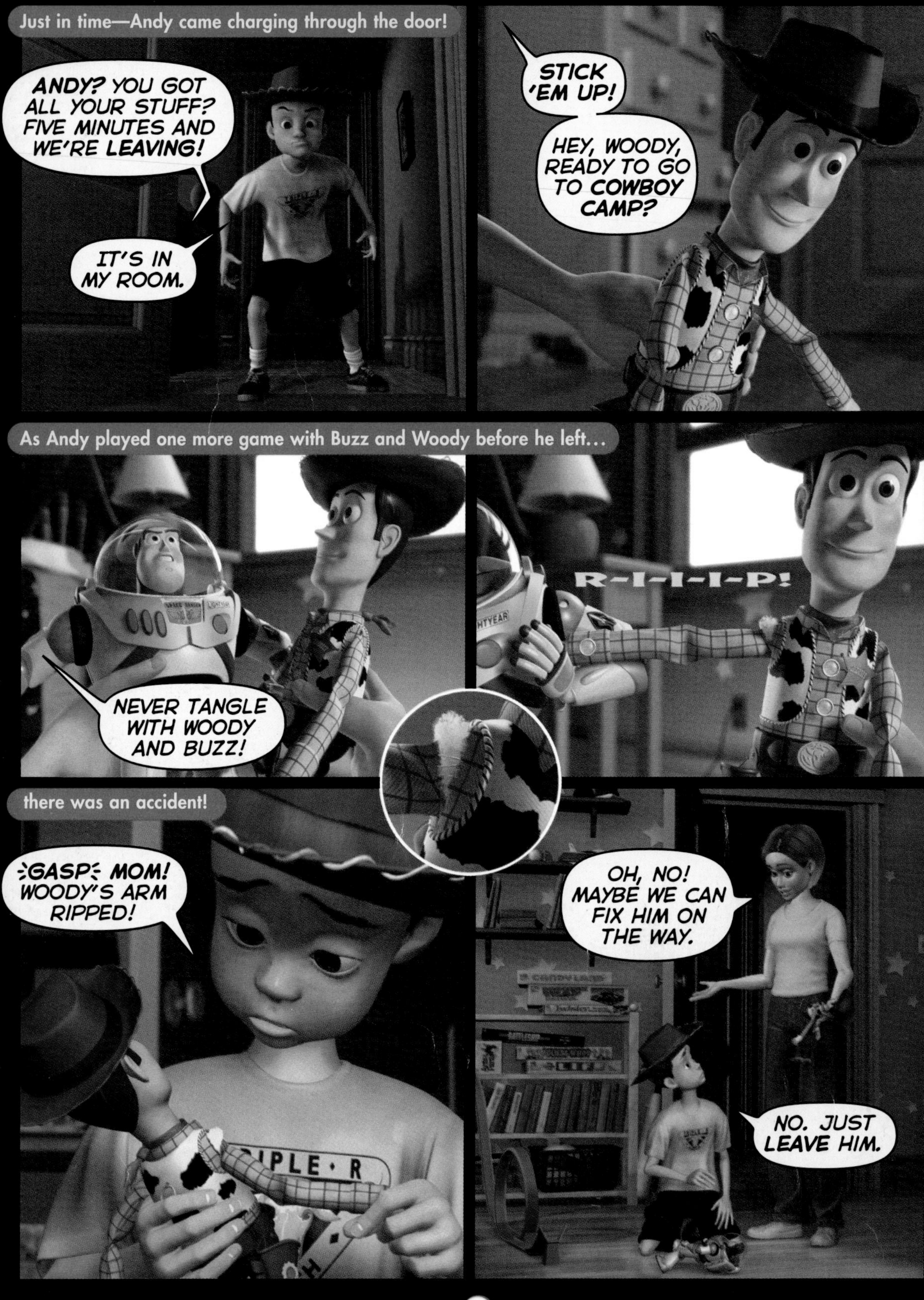

Just in time—Andy came charging through the door!
ANDY? YOU GOT ALL YOUR STUFF? FIVE MINUTES AND WE'RE LEAVING!
IT'S IN MY ROOM.
STICK 'EM UP!
HEY, WOODY, READY TO GO TO COWBOY CAMP?
As Andy played one more game with Buzz and Woody before he left...
NEVER TANGLE WITH WOODY AND BUZZ!
R-I-I-I-P!
there was an accident!
GASP MOM! WOODY'S ARM RIPPED!
OH, NO! MAYBE WE CAN FIX HIM ON THE WAY.
NO. JUST LEAVE HIM.

Andy's mom put Woody up on a shelf in his room.
I'M SORRY, HONEY, BUT YOU KNOW, TOYS DON'T LAST FOREVER!
With Andy gone, the toys jumped up!
WHAT HAPPENED?
WOODY'S BEEN SHELVED!
ANDY!
Woody was in shock! Andy was going to Cowboy Camp without him!

The next morning...Andy's back early from Cowboy Camp?

Woody fell...and FELL...for a VERY long time.

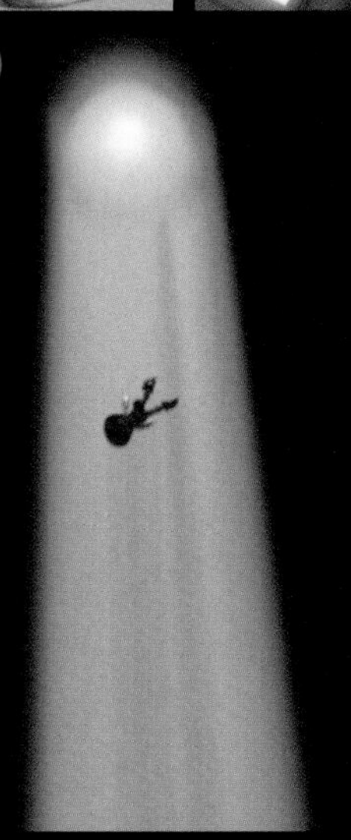

Woody woke up from his nightmare.

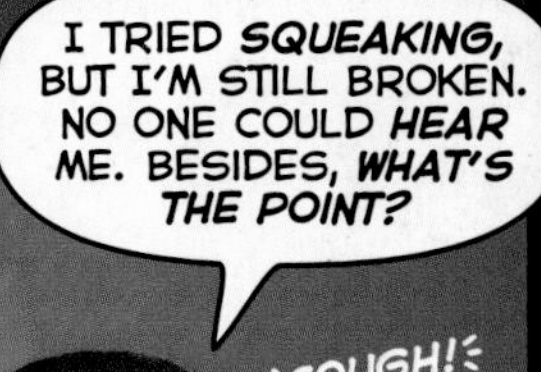

THERE!
A YARD SALE? YARD SALE!
GUYS! WAKE UP! THERE'S A YARD SALE OUTSIDE! SARGE! EMERGENCY ROLL CALL!
RED ALERT! ALL CIVILIANS FALL INTO POSITION! NOW!
HAMM?
HERE!
MR. AND MRS. POTATO HEAD?
HERE!
TROIKAS? CHECK!
SLINKY?
YO!
REX?
OH, I HATE YARD SALES.
AH! SOMEONE'S COMING!
The toys all resumed their places as Andy's mom came into the room carrying a big empty box.
25¢

BYE, WOODY!
GASP!
Woody wouldn't give up on his old pal.
TWEET!
So he whistled for Andy's dog, Buster!
OKAY, BOY, TO THE YARD SALE! YAW!
WOODY!
DON'T DO IT, WOODY! WE LOVE YOU!
WHAT'S HE DOING? HIS ARM AIN'T THAT BAD!
PANT PANT
OKAY, BOY, LET'S GO. AND KEEP IT CASUAL.
25¢
CAN YOU SEE HIM?
THERE HE IS!
WOODY, YOU'RE WORTH MORE THAN THAT.
HE'S SELLING HIMSELF FOR 25 CENTS!?
HEY! IT'S NOT SUICIDE! IT'S A RESCUE!

BLESS YOU, WOODY.
THERE YOU GO, PAL. ALL RIGHT NOW, BACK TO ANDY'S ROOM.
On the way back...
WOODY FELL OFF!
UH-OH.
MOMMY, LOOK, A COWBOY DOLLY. CAN WE GET HIM?
HONEY, WE'RE NOT BUYING BROKEN TOYS.
Then...
ORIGINAL FACE, BLANKET-STITCHED VEST...
HMMM, A LITTLE RIP...FIXABLE.
OH, I FOUND HIM! I FOUND HIM!

EXCUSE ME, CAN I HELP YOU?
AH, I'LL GIVE YOU FIFTY CENTS FOR THIS JUNK.
OH, A PRO, AYE? VERY WELL, FIVE DOLLARS.
OH, NOW HOW DID THIS GET DOWN HERE?
JUST HAND HER THE SHERIFF, NICE AND EASY.
I'M SORRY. IT'S AN OLD FAMILY TOY.
WAIT! I'LL GIVE YOU FIFTY BUCKS FOR HIM!
IT'S NOT FOR SALE.
BUT, BUT, LADY!
PHEW! THAT WAS CLOSE!
FIFTY BUCKS AIN'T BAD.
OH, NO! HE'S STEALING WOODY!
WHERE'S HE GOING?

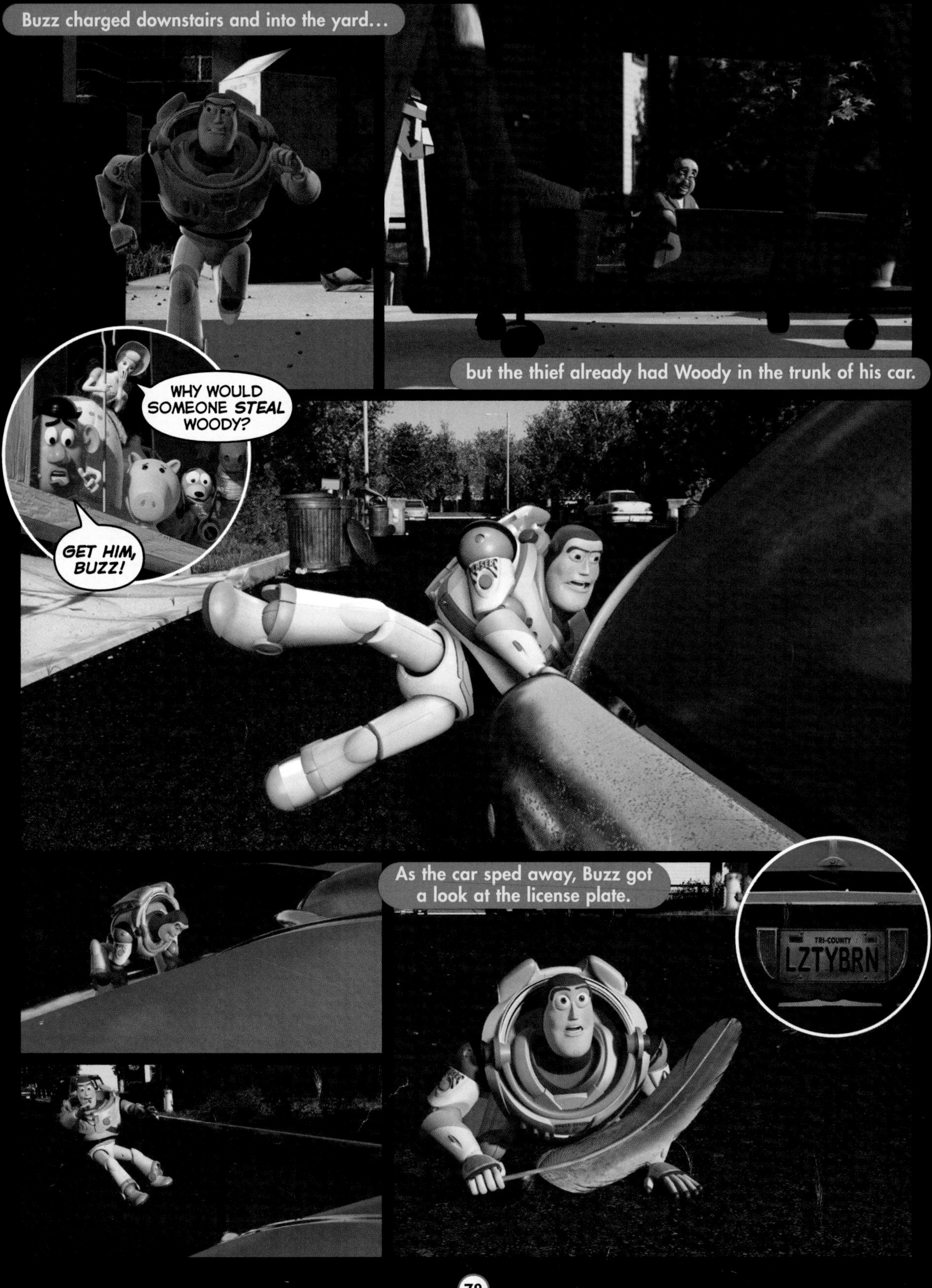

Buzz charged downstairs and into the yard...

but the thief already had Woody in the trunk of his car.



As the car sped away, Buzz got a look at the license plate.

Later...
ALL RIGHT, LET'S REVIEW THIS ONE MORE TIME.
AT PRECISELY 8:32-ISH, WOODY WAS KIDNAPPED. HERE'S THE COMPOSITE SKETCH OF THE KIDNAPPER.
OH, PICKY, PICKY, PICKY.
HE WAS BIGGER THAN THAT!
I KNOW HE WORE GLASSES.
DIDN'T HE WEAR GLASSES?
EXCUSE ME! A LITTLE QUIET, PLEASE? THANK YOU!
HUH?
THERE'S A MESSAGE ENCODED IN THAT VEHICLE'S ID TAG. HMMM...
LOUSY TRY BR
LAZY TOY BRAIN
LOUSY TRY BRIAN
LIZ TRY BRAN
LOU'S THIGH BURN
LOU'S THIGH BURN
HMM! TOY? "TOY!" HOLD ON!
AL'S TOY BARN
AL'S TOY BARN?

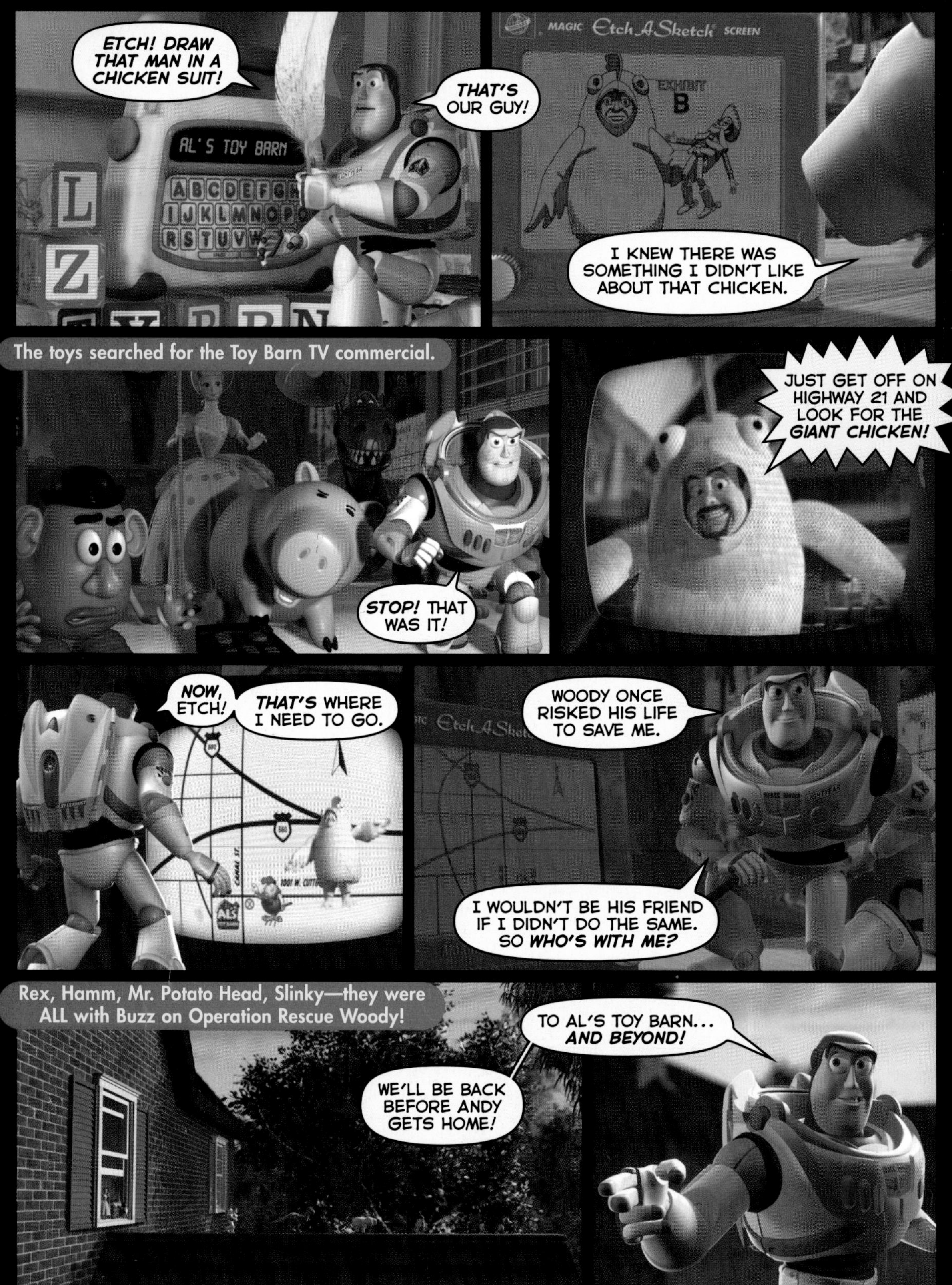
ETCH! DRAW THAT MAN IN A CHICKEN SUIT!
AL'S TOY BARN
THAT'S OUR GUY!
MAGIC Etch A Sketch SCREEN
EXHIBIT B
I KNEW THERE WAS SOMETHING I DIDN'T LIKE ABOUT THAT CHICKEN.
The toys searched for the Toy Barn TV commercial.
STOP! THAT WAS IT!
JUST GET OFF ON HIGHWAY 21 AND LOOK FOR THE GIANT CHICKEN!
NOW, ETCH!
THAT'S WHERE I NEED TO GO.
WOODY ONCE RISKED HIS LIFE TO SAVE ME.
I WOULDN'T BE HIS FRIEND IF I DIDN'T DO THE SAME. SO WHO'S WITH ME?
Rex, Hamm, Mr. Potato Head, Slinky—they were ALL with Buzz on Operation Rescue Woody!
TO AL'S TOY BARN... AND BEYOND!
WE'LL BE BACK BEFORE ANDY GETS HOME!

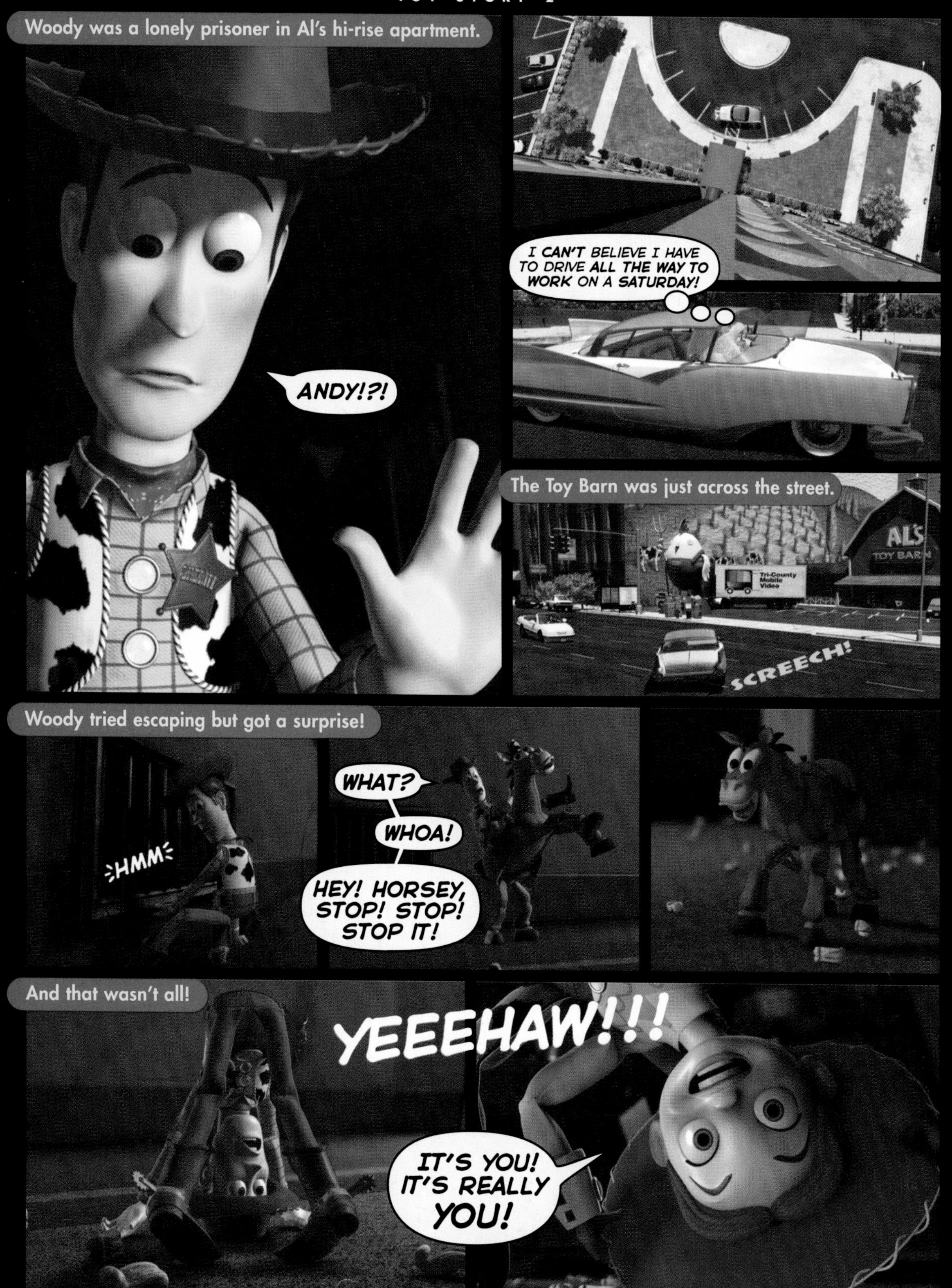
Woody was a lonely prisoner in Al's hi-rise apartment.
ANDY!?!
I CAN'T BELIEVE I HAVE TO DRIVE ALL THE WAY TO WORK ON A SATURDAY!
The Toy Barn was just across the street.
AL'S
TOY BARN
Tri-County Mobile Video
SCREECH!
Woody tried escaping but got a surprise!
HMM
WHAT?
WHOA!
HEY! HORSEY, STOP! STOP! STOP IT!
And that wasn't all!
YEEEHAW!!!
IT'S YOU! IT'S REALLY YOU!

IT'S YOU! IT'S REALLY YOU!
WHAT'S ME?
WHOO-WEE!
The girl yanked Woody's voice box string.
HA! IT IS YOU!
THERE'S A SNAKE IN MY BOOT!
PLEASE STOP SAYING THAT.
PROSPECTOR SAID SOME DAY YOU'D COME! HE'LL WANT TO MEETCHA!
TV
STINKY PETE
HE'S MINT IN THE BOX. NEVER BEEN OPENED!
WHY, THE PRODIGAL SON HAS RETURNED!
IT'S GOOD TO SEE YOU, WOODY.
AS SEEN ON TV
OKAY, I'M OFFICIALLY FREAKED OUT NOW. HOW DO YOU KNOW MY NAME?
WHY, YOU DON'T KNOW WHO YOU ARE, DO YOU?
Bullseye turned up the lights to reveal...
a room full of Woody memorabilia!
Woody
ROUNDUP
Hey Howdy Hey!
THAT'S ME!
WOW!

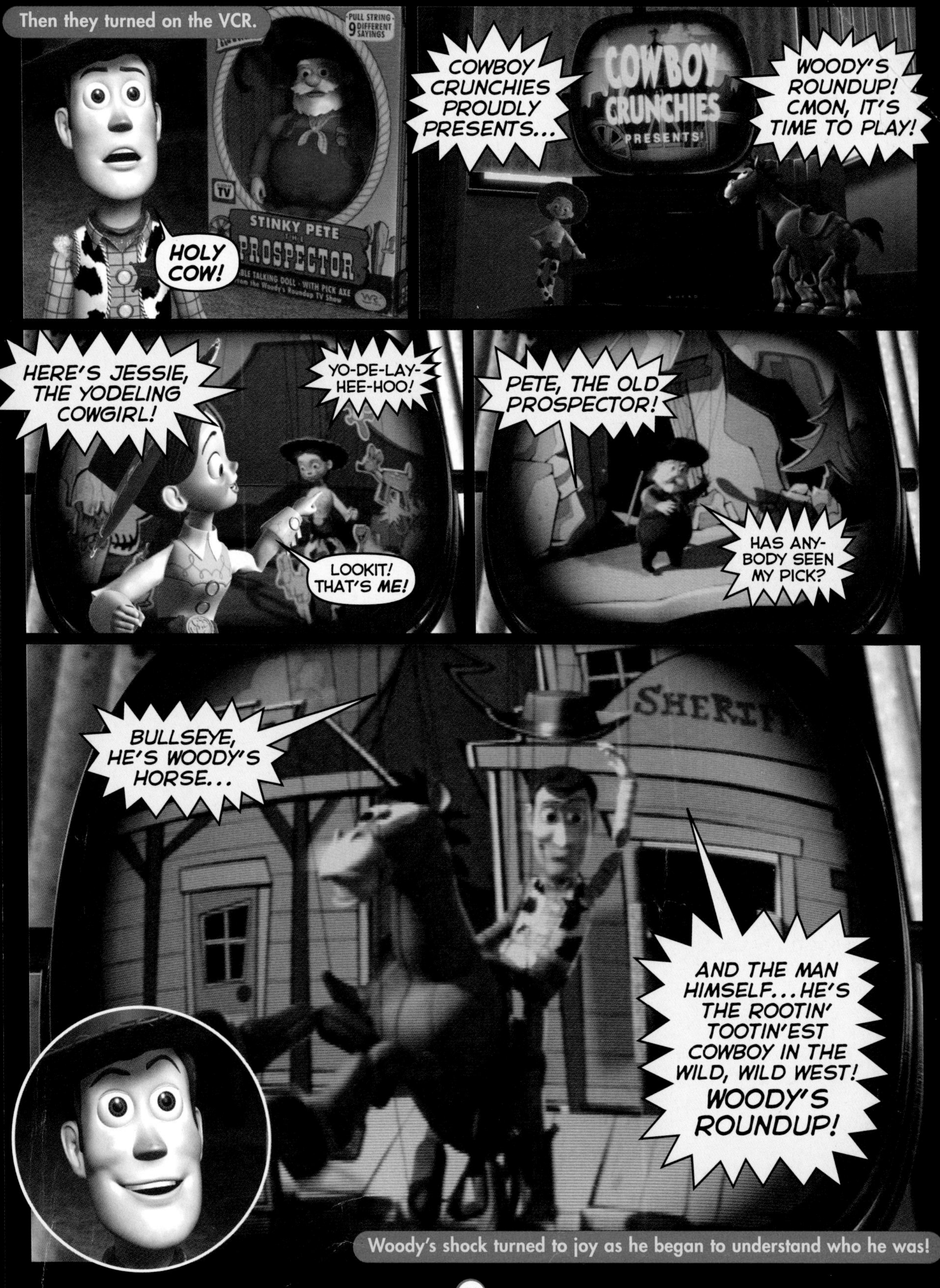

Then they turned on the VCR.

BULLSEYE, HE'S WOODY'S HORSE...

AND THE MAN HIMSELF...HE'S THE ROOTIN' TOOTIN'EST COWBOY IN THE WILD, WILD WEST! **WOODY'S ROUNDUP!**

Woody's shock turned to joy as he began to understand who he was!

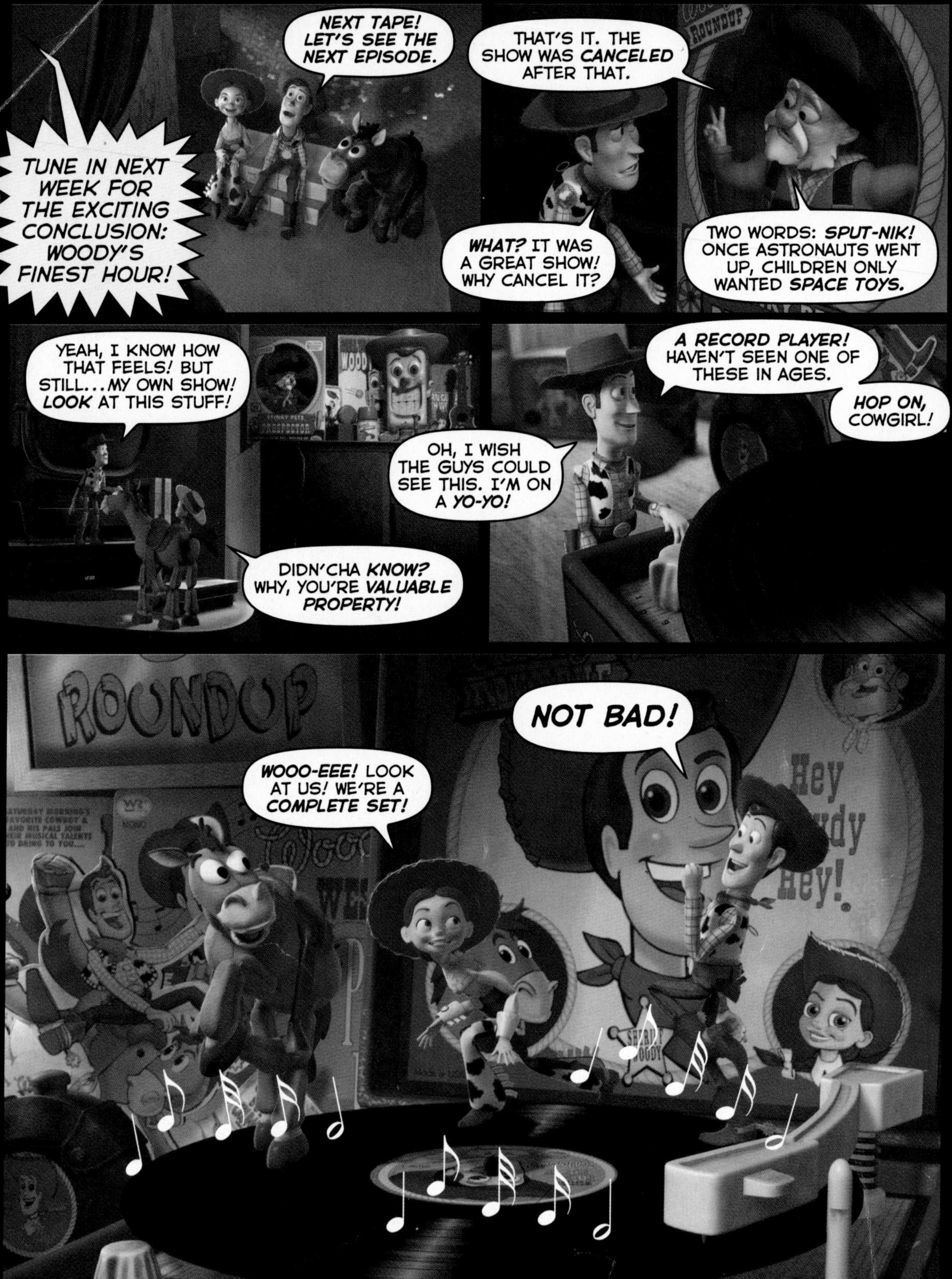

TUNE IN NEXT WEEK FOR THE EXCITING CONCLUSION: WOODY'S FINEST HOUR!
NEXT TAPE! LET'S SEE THE NEXT EPISODE.
THAT'S IT. THE SHOW WAS CANCELED AFTER THAT.
WHAT? IT WAS A GREAT SHOW! WHY CANCEL IT?
TWO WORDS: SPUT-NIK! ONCE ASTRONAUTS WENT UP, CHILDREN ONLY WANTED SPACE TOYS.
YEAH, I KNOW HOW THAT FEELS! BUT STILL...MY OWN SHOW! LOOK AT THIS STUFF!
DIDN'CHA KNOW? WHY, YOU'RE VALUABLE PROPERTY!
OH, I WISH THE GUYS COULD SEE THIS. I'M ON A YO-YO!
A RECORD PLAYER! HAVEN'T SEEN ONE OF THESE IN AGES.
HOP ON, COWGIRL!
WOOO-EEE! LOOK AT US! WE'RE A COMPLETE SET!
NOT BAD!

NOW IT'S ON TO THE MUSEUM!
MUSEUM? WHAT MUSEUM?
WE'RE BEING SOLD TO THE KONISHI TOY MUSEUM IN TOKYO!
STINKY PETE THE PROSPECTOR
THAT'S IN JAPAN!
JAPAN? NO, NO, NO. I CAN'T GO TO JAPAN. I GOTTA GET HOME TO MY OWNER, ANDY.
OH, MY GOODNESS!
HE STILL HAS AN OWNER?
NO! I CAN'T DO STORAGE AGAIN. I JUST CAN'T.
WHAT'S THE MATTER?
WE'VE BEEN IN STORAGE A LONG TIME, WOODY– WAITING FOR YOU.
IT'S NOT FAIR! HOW CAN YOU DO THIS TO US?
THE MUSEUM'S ONLY INTERESTED IN THE COLLECTION IF YOU'RE IN IT, WOODY.
WITHOUT YOU, WE GO BACK IN STORAGE. IT'S THAT SIMPLE.
I'M SORRY, BUT THIS IS ALL A BIG MISTAKE.
I'M NOT GOING TO ANY MUSEUM.
WELL, I'M NOT GOING BACK INTO STORAGE!
AL'S COMING!

IT'S SHOW TIME!
OH, HO, HO! MONEY, MONEY, MONEY!
AND NOW THE MAIN ATTRACTION.
Whoops—not again!
R-I-I-I-P!
AAAAH! HIS ARM! WHERE'S HIS ARM?
WHAT AM I GOING TO DO? OH! I KNOW!
Al went off to call—The Cleaner!
Woody's ROUNDUP
LUCKY?! ARE YOU SHRINK-WRAPPED? I'M MISSING MY ARM!
IT'S JUST A POPPED SEAM. YOU SHOULD CONSIDER YOUR-SELF LUCKY.
IT'S A DANGEROUS WORLD OUT THERE FOR A TOY.
PULL STRING 9 DIFFERENT SAYINGS
Prospector had a point. Museums were SAFER!

Late that night, as Al slept…
ZZZZZZZZZZZZZZZ
KRUNCH!
BULLSEYE! DON'T HELP ME! I'M THE BAD GUY!
YOU'RE GONNA GO BACK IN STORAGE BECAUSE OF ME, REMEMBER?
ALL RIGHT, BUT YOU HAVE GOT TO KEEP QUIET! NOW C'MON!

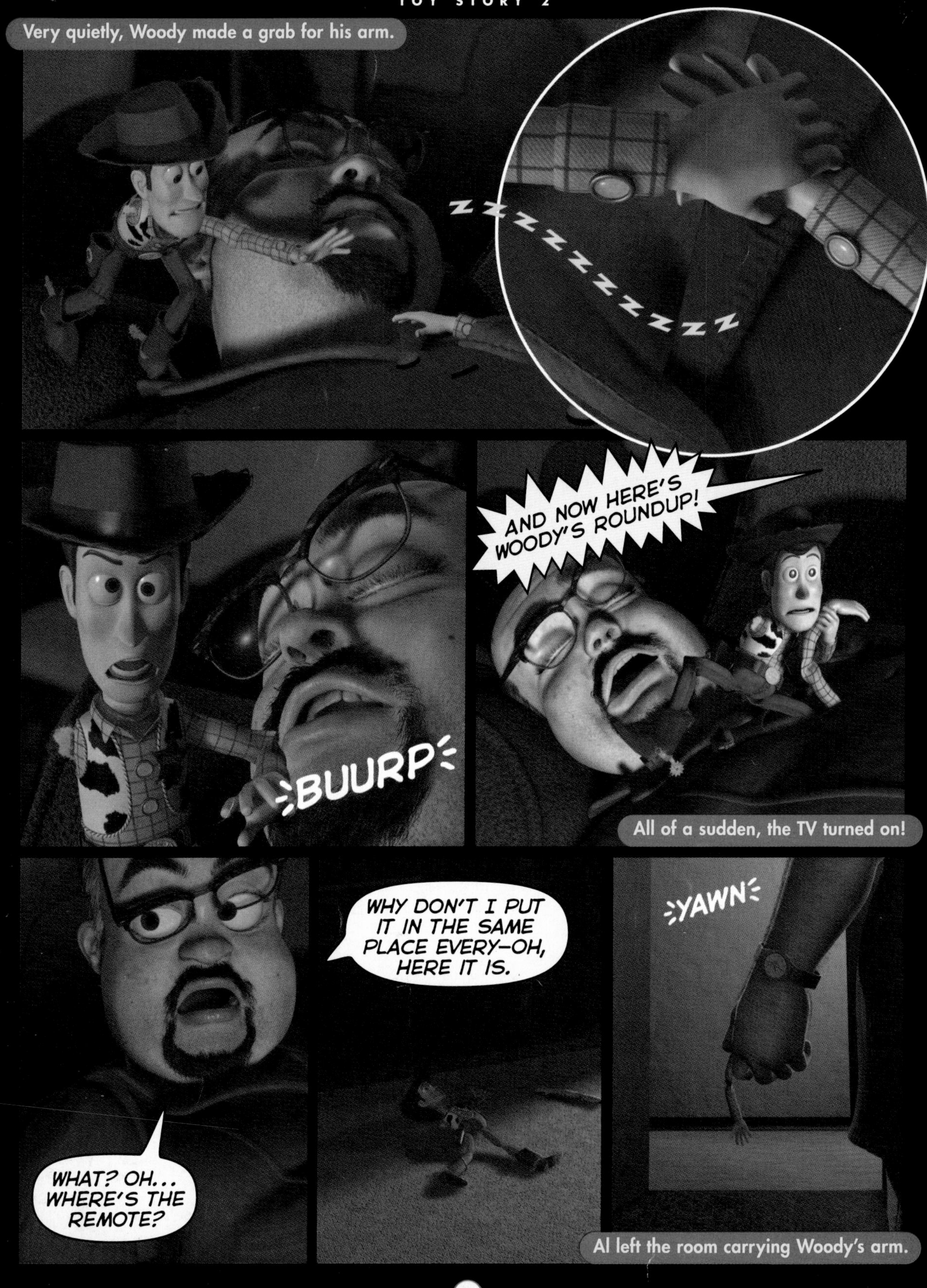
Very quietly, Woody made a grab for his arm.
ZZZZZZZZZZZZZZZ
BUURP
AND NOW HERE'S WOODY'S ROUNDUP!
All of a sudden, the TV turned on!
WHAT? OH... WHERE'S THE REMOTE?
WHY DON'T I PUT IT IN THE SAME PLACE EVERY—OH, HERE IT IS.
YAWN
Al left the room carrying Woody's arm.

WHAT IS YOUR PROBLEM? YOU DIDN'T HAVE TO PULL A STUNT LIKE THAT!
WHAT? YOU THINK I TURNED ON THE TV?
OH, RIGHT. THE TV JUST HAPPENED TO TURN ON AND THE REMOTE MAGICALLY ENDED UP IN FRONT OF YOU.
POSEABLE TALKING DOLL · WITH PICK AXE
From the Woody's Roundup TV Show
ARE YOU CALLING ME A LIAR?
OKAY, COWBOY! HOW DO YOU LIKE THAT!
WELL, IF THE BOOT FITS–
TAKE IT BACK!
DON'T THINK THAT JUST BECAUSE YOU'RE A GIRL I'M GONNA TAKE IT EASY ON YOU.
AAAAAGH!
JESSIE! WOODY! STOP THIS AT ONCE!
PULL STRING 9 DIFFERENT SAYINGS
SEE? HE DOESN'T EVEN BELIEVE YOU.
PULL STRING 9 DIFFERENT SAYINGS
TELL THAT SORRY EXCUSE FOR A COWBOY THAT I DID NOT TURN ON THE TV.
NOW, JESSIE, I'M SURE YOU DIDN'T, BUT–
POSEABLE TALKING DOLL · WITH PICK AXE
From the Woody's Roundup TV Show
I DON'T KNOW HOW THAT TV TURNED ON, BUT FIGHTING ISN'T HELPING ANYTHING.

Woody's ROUNDUP
PULL STRING 9 DIFFERENT SAYINGS
AS SEEN ON TV
IF I HAD *BOTH* MY ARMS...
WELL, *YOU DON'T*, WOODY. SO I SUGGEST YOU WAIT UNTIL MORNING. *THE CLEANER* WILL COME, FIX YOUR ARM, AND...
*AND THEN I'M OUT OF HERE.*
NO, NO, BULLSEYE– DON'T TAKE IT THAT WAY.
IT'S JUST THAT ANDY–
*ANDY! ANDY! ANDY!* THAT'S ALL HE EVER *TALKS* ABOUT.
STINKY PE
PROSPECT
POSEABLE TALKING DOLL · WITH PI
From the Woody's Roundup TV S

After marching all night...
LOSING HEALTH UNITS... MUST...REST.
IS EVERYONE PRESENT AND ACCOUNTED FOR?
NOT QUITE EVERYONE.
WHO'S BEHIND?
MINE!
AL'S TOY BARN!
YA-HOO!
HEY, GUYS! WHY DID THE TOYS CROSS THE ROAD?
TO GET TO THE CHICKEN ON THE OTHER SIDE!
AL'S
TOY BARN
They had made it!

All they had to do was get across the street!

BEEP!
BEEP!

WE'LL HAVE TO CROSS. THERE *MUST* BE A SAFE WAY.

I MIGHT NOT BE A SMART DOG, BUT I KNOW WHAT *ROADKILL* IS!

YOU'RE *NOT* TURNING *ME* INTO A MASHED POTATO.

OKAY, HERE'S OUR CHANCE! *GO!*

SCREEEEECH

*NOW DROP!*

*GOOD JOB,* TROOPS. WE'RE THAT MUCH CLOSER TO WOODY.

POP!

High above Buzz and the gang, The Cleaner arrived.

Woody was as good as new. Al couldn't wait any longer.

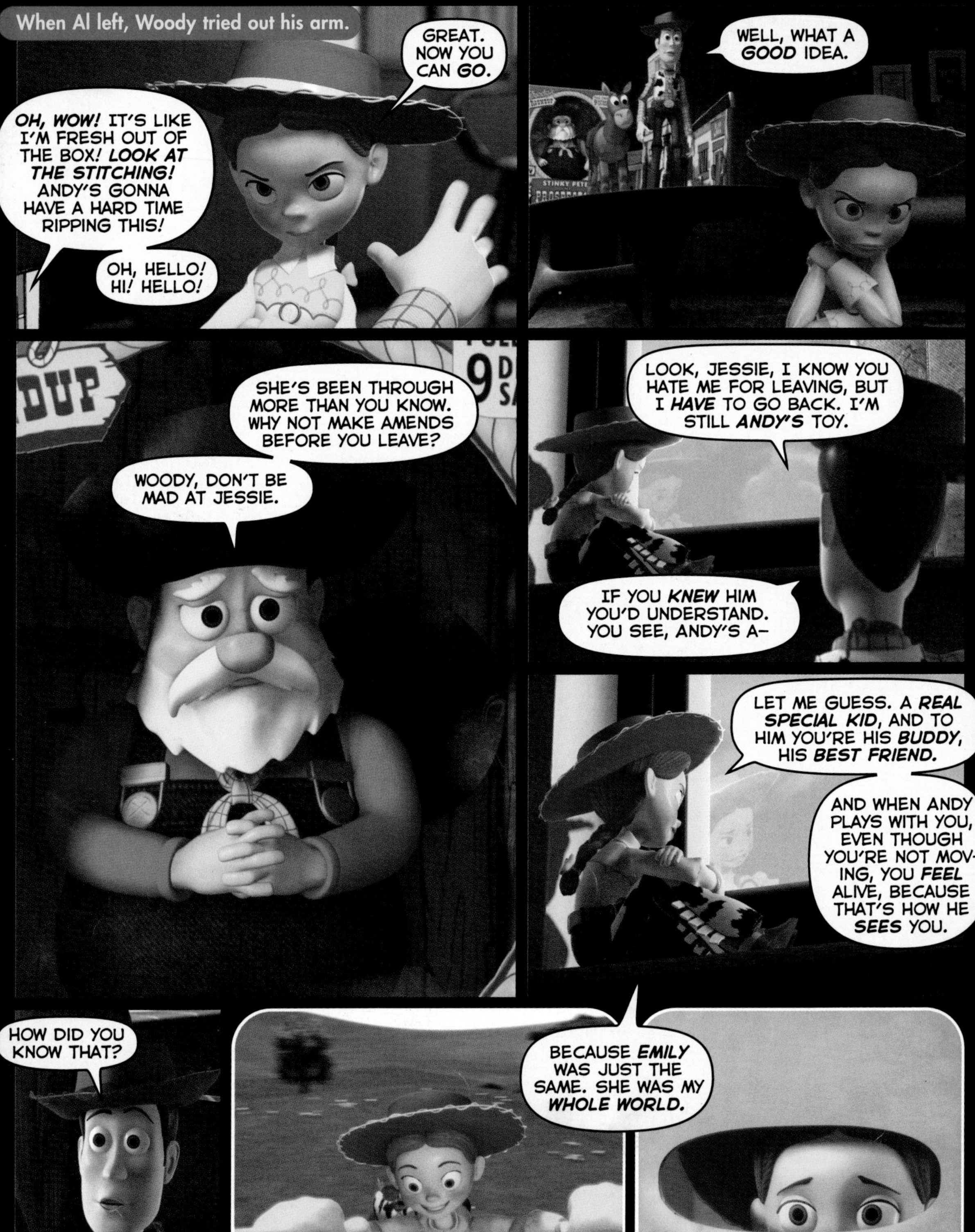
When Al left, Woody tried out his arm.
GREAT. NOW YOU CAN GO.
OH, WOW! IT'S LIKE I'M FRESH OUT OF THE BOX! LOOK AT THE STITCHING! ANDY'S GONNA HAVE A HARD TIME RIPPING THIS!
OH, HELLO! HI! HELLO!
WELL, WHAT A GOOD IDEA.
STINKY PETE
SHE'S BEEN THROUGH MORE THAN YOU KNOW. WHY NOT MAKE AMENDS BEFORE YOU LEAVE?
WOODY, DON'T BE MAD AT JESSIE.
LOOK, JESSIE, I KNOW YOU HATE ME FOR LEAVING, BUT I HAVE TO GO BACK. I'M STILL ANDY'S TOY.
IF YOU KNEW HIM YOU'D UNDERSTAND. YOU SEE, ANDY'S A–
LET ME GUESS. A REAL SPECIAL KID, AND TO HIM YOU'RE HIS BUDDY, HIS BEST FRIEND.
AND WHEN ANDY PLAYS WITH YOU, EVEN THOUGH YOU'RE NOT MOVING, YOU FEEL ALIVE, BECAUSE THAT'S HOW HE SEES YOU.
HOW DID YOU KNOW THAT?
BECAUSE EMILY WAS JUST THE SAME. SHE WAS MY WHOLE WORLD.

YOU NEVER FORGET KIDS LIKE EMILY, OR ANDY.
BUT THEY FORGET YOU.
DONATIONS
TRI-COUNTY CHARITIES
Woody opened the air grate, then paused.
JUST GO.
JESSIE, I-I DIDN'T KNOW.
HOW LONG WILL IT LAST, WOODY? DO YOU REALLY THINK ANDY IS GOING TO TAKE YOU TO COLLEGE? OR ON HIS HONEYMOON?
ANDY'S GROWING UP, AND THERE'S NOTHING YOU CAN DO ABOUT IT.
IT'S YOUR CHOICE, WOODY. YOU CAN GO BACK, OR YOU CAN STAY WITH US AND BE ADORED BY CHILDREN FOR GENERATIONS.
WHO AM I TO BREAK UP THE ROUNDUP GANG?
!?!

Outside the rescue team approached Al's Toy Barn, which was about to open.

AL'S
TOY BARN

Jumping up and down on the mat, the toys triggered the electric doors.

Sorry WE'RE CLOSED

ALL TOGETHER!

The toys split up to see what they could find…

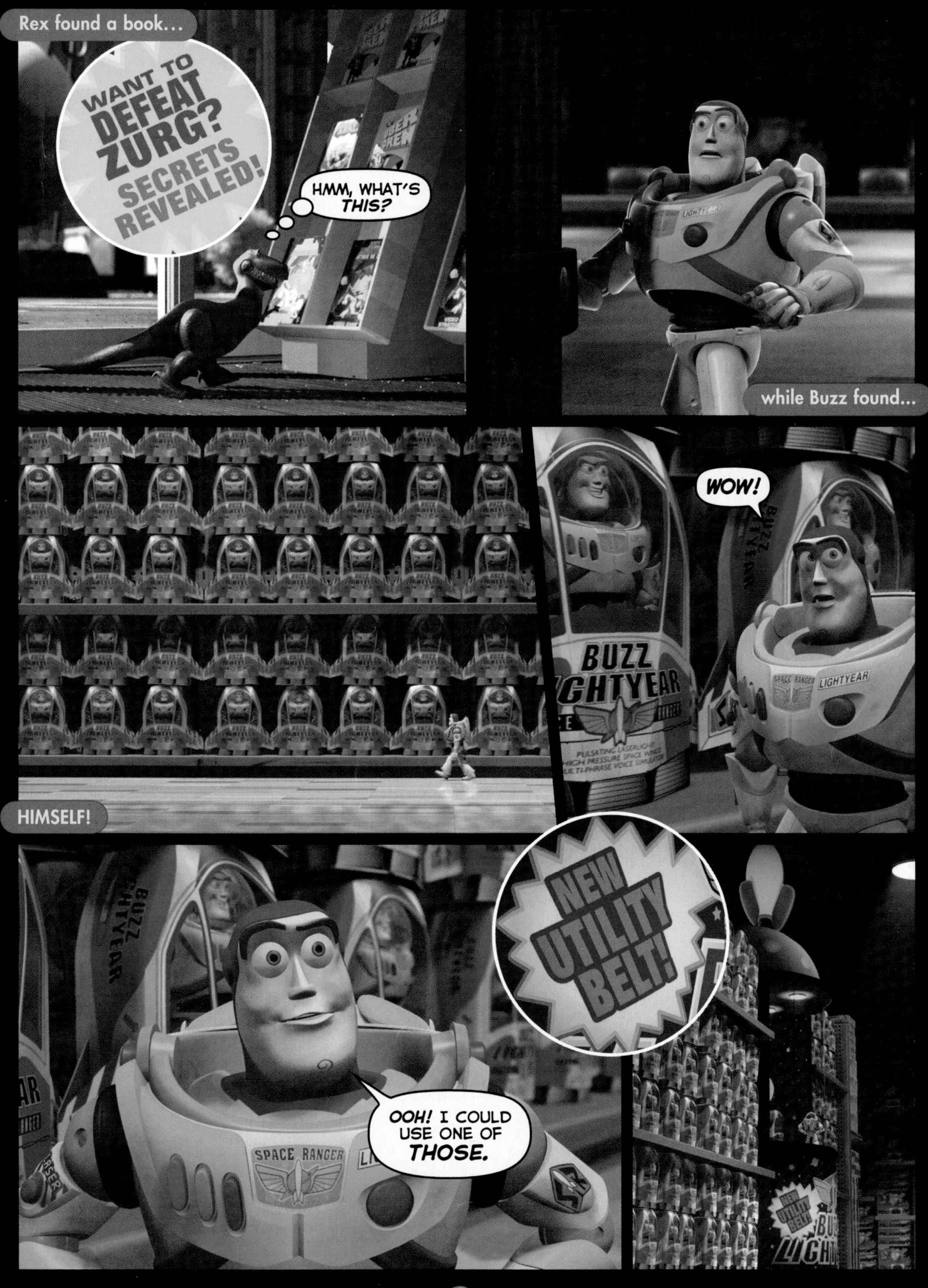
Rex found a book...
WANT TO DEFEAT ZURG? SECRETS REVEALED!
HMM, WHAT'S THIS?
while Buzz found...
HIMSELF!
WOW!
BUZZ LIGHTYEAR
OOH! I COULD USE ONE OF THOSE.
NEW UTILITY BELT!

Suddenly...
HO-YAAAH!
YOU'RE IN DIRECT VIOLATION OF CODE 6404.5, STATING ALL SPACE RANGERS ARE TO BE IN *HYPER-SLEEP* UNTIL AWAKENED BY AUTHORIZED PERSONNEL.
OW! WHAT ARE YOU DOING?
BUZZ LIGHTYEAR

YOU'RE BREAKING RANKS, RANGER!
OH, NO! TELL ME I WASN'T *THIS* DELUDED.

NO BACK TALK. I HAVE A LASER AND I WILL USE IT.
UNH!

YOU MEAN THE LASER THAT'S A *LIGHTBULB?*
BZZZAAAP!
HAS YOUR MIND BEEN *MELDED?* YOU COULD HAVE *KILLED* ME, SPACE RANGER.

OR SHOULD I SAY, *"TRAITOR"*?
HALT! I ORDER YOU TO HALT!
BZZZAAAP!
I DON'T HAVE *TIME* FOR THIS.

Over in the other aisle, the toys kept up the search.

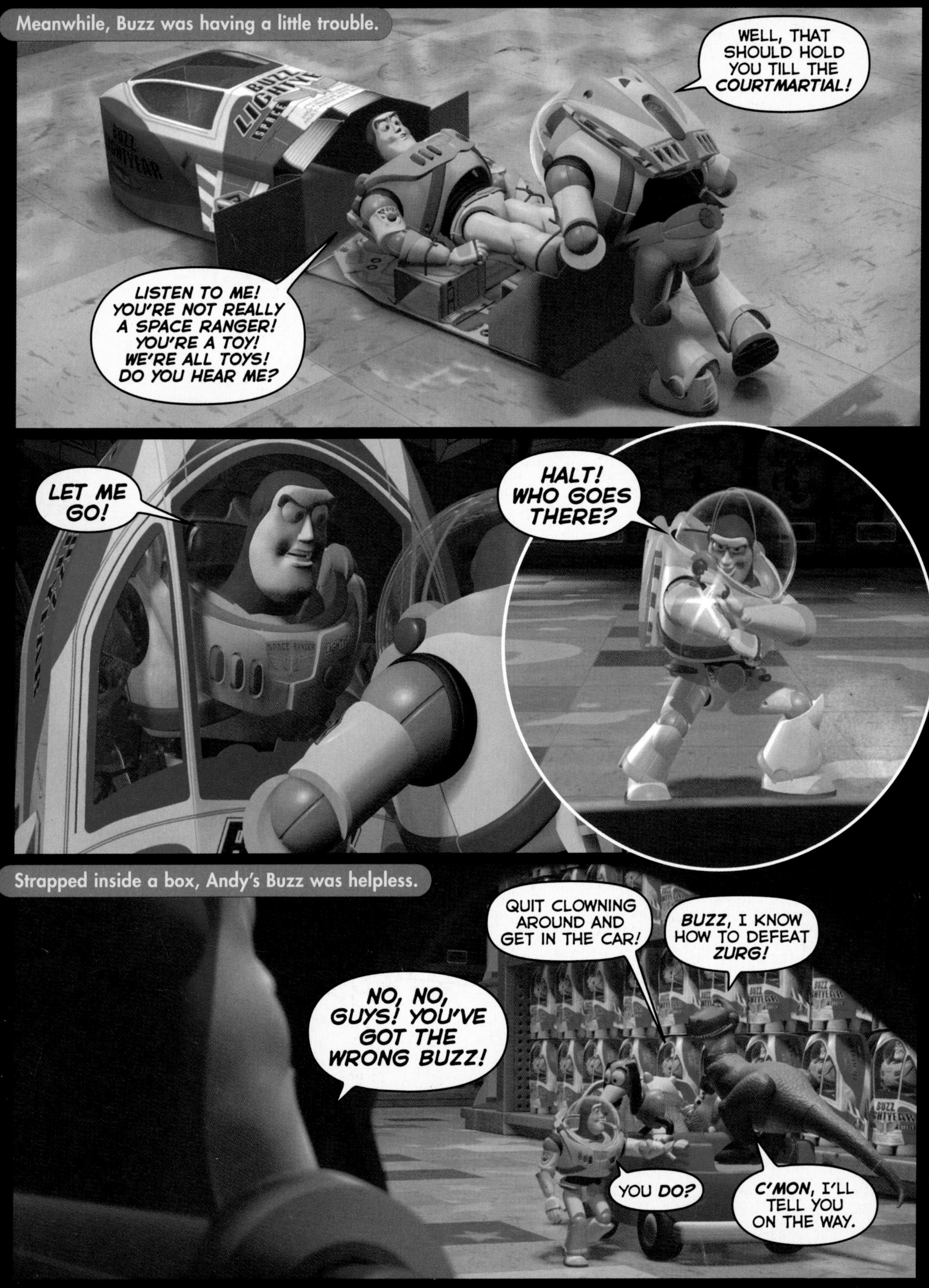
Meanwhile, Buzz was having a little trouble.
WELL, THAT SHOULD HOLD YOU TILL THE COURTMARTIAL!
LISTEN TO ME! YOU'RE NOT REALLY A SPACE RANGER! YOU'RE A TOY! WE'RE ALL TOYS! DO YOU HEAR ME?
LET ME GO!
HALT! WHO GOES THERE?
Strapped inside a box, Andy's Buzz was helpless.
NO, NO, GUYS! YOU'VE GOT THE WRONG BUZZ!
QUIT CLOWNING AROUND AND GET IN THE CAR!
BUZZ, I KNOW HOW TO DEFEAT ZURG!
YOU DO?
C'MON, I'LL TELL YOU ON THE WAY.

Leaving Andy's Buzz behind, the toys found their way into Al's office.

ALL ALONG WE THOUGHT THE WAY INTO ZURG'S FORTRESS WAS THROUGH THE MAIN GATE. BUT *IN FACT* THE SECRET ENTRANCE IS TO THE LEFT, *HIDDEN IN THE SHADOWS.*

TO THE LEFT AND IN THE SHADOWS. *GOT IT.*

*WOODY?*

*HEY, WOODY! WOODY!*

*WOODY, ARE YOU IN HERE?*

*MOSHI, MOSHI, KONISHI-SAN. YES, I'M AT MY OFFICE.*

*SHHH... SOMEONE'S COMING!*

*EVERYONE! TAKE COVER!*

*NOW, LET ME CONFIRM YOUR FAX NUMBER.*

*ALL RIGHT. THAT'S A LOT OF NUMBERS!*

*IT'S HIM!*

*THE CHICKEN MAN!*

AN AGENT OF *ZURG* IF I EVER SAW ONE.

*AND NOW FOR THE PIÈCE DE RÉSISTANCE...*

*IT'S WOODY!*

Meanwhile...

Andy's Buzz escaped just in time to see Al heading for his car—with a briefcase full of stowaways.

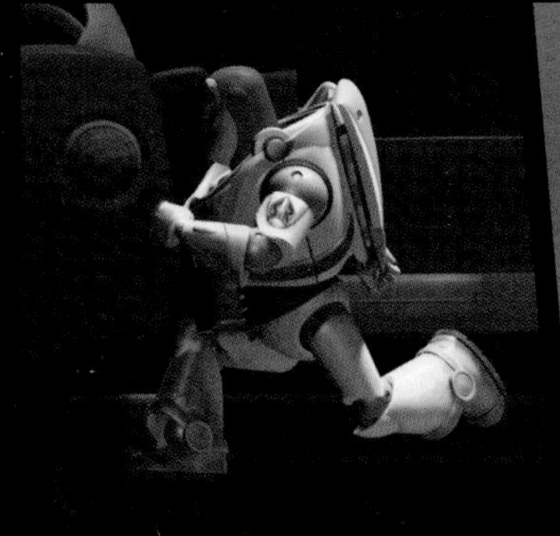

BOING!

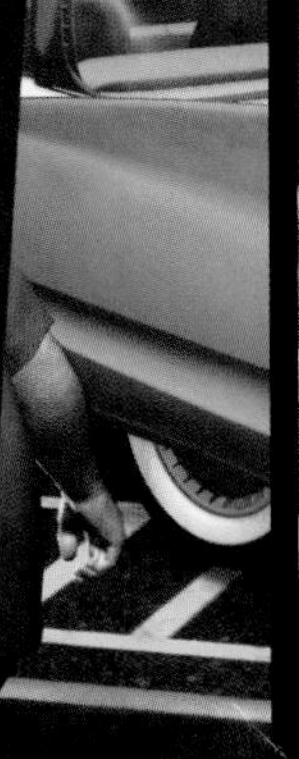

The front door closed just as Buzz got to it.

Buzz sent a stack of boxes crashing down on the electric doormat.
ARRH!
As the doors shut again, one box was caught. Out popped…
EVIL EMPEROR
ZURG
ARCH ENEMY OF
EVIL EMPEROR
GRRR
ZURG VISION
DESTROY BUZZ LIGHTYEAR.
DESTROY BUZZ LIGHTYEAR.
Buzz followed Al. Zurg followed Buzz.

Al went into the building, leaving New Buzz and the others in the car.
NO TIME TO LOSE! ALL RIGHT, EVERY-ONE, HANG ON! WE'RE GOING TO BLAST THROUGH THE ROOF!
UH, BUZZ?
WHAT ARE YOU, INSANE!
TO INFINITY... AND BEYOND!
I DON'T UNDERSTAND! MY FUEL TANKS HAVE GONE DRY!
New Buzz accidently leaned on the switch, springing open the door.
He rushed to the entrance just as Al got into the elevator.
HE'S ASCENDING IN THE VERTICAL TRANSPORTER!

BLAST! HE'S ON LEVEL 23!
HOW ARE WE GOING TO GET UP THERE?
MAYBE IF WE FIND SOME BALLOONS, WE COULD FLOAT TO THE TOP.
ARE YOU KIDDING? I SAY WE STACK OURSELVES UP, PUSH THE INTERCOM, AND PRETEND WE'RE DELIVERING A PIZZA!
HOW 'BOUT A HAM SANDWICH?
WITH FRIES AND A HOT DOG.
WHAT ABOUT ME?
ER, YOU CAN BE THE TOY THAT COMES WITH THE MEAL.
TROOPS! OVER HERE!
JUST LIKE YOU SAID, LIZARD MAN: IN THE SHADOWS, TO THE LEFT.
MISSION LOG: HAVE INFILTRATED ENEMY TERRITORY WITHOUT DETECTION, AND ARE MAKING OUR WAY THROUGH ZURG'S FORTRESS!
OH, NO! WHICH WAY DO WE GO?
THIS WAY!
WHAT MAKES YOU SO SURE?
I'M BUZZ LIGHTYEAR. I'M ALWAYS SURE.

They had stumbled into the elevator shaft.
THOCK!
THOCK!
COME ON! WE'VE GOT NO TIME TO LOSE. EVERYONE GRAB HOLD.
UH, BUZZ? WHY NOT JUST TAKE THE ELEVATOR?
THEY'LL BE EXPECTING THAT.
THOCK!
THOCK!
MY ARMS CAN'T HOLD ON MUCH LONGER!
HEY! WHOA! AHHHH!
KLUNK!
TOO... HEAVY!
BUZZ! BUZZ! HELP!

New Buzz was losing his grip!
WHAT WAS I THINKING? MY ANTIGRAVITY SERVOS!
HANG TIGHT, EVERYONE! I AM GOING TO LET GO OF THE WALL!
HE WOULD!
WHAT? HE WOULDN'T!
NO-O-O!
ONE!
TWO!
THREE!
TO INFINITY AND... BEYOND!
YAAAH!
Just then, the elevator rose beneath them.
APPROACHING DESTINATION.
REENGAGING GRAVITY.
KLUNK!
KLUNK!
AREA SECURE!
GROAN!
IT'S OKAY, TROOPS. THE ANTIGRAVITY SICKNESS WILL WEAR OFF MOMENTARILY. NOW...LET'S MOVE!
REMIND ME TO GLUE HIS HELMET SHUT WHEN WE GET BACK.
Underneath the elevator...
Andy's Buzz was right behind!

Inside Al's apartment...

DOLLARS? YOU ARE DELIBERATELY TAKING ADVANTAGE OF PEOPLE, YOU KNOW THAT?

TO OVERNIGHT PACKAGES TO JAPAN IS HOW MUCH?

WHAT?!? THAT'S IN YEN, RIGHT?

ALL RIGHT, I'LL DO IT! ALL RIGHT, FINE.

I'LL HAVE THE STUFF IN THE LOBBY. YOU'D BETTER BE HERE IN FIFTEEN MINUTES, 'CAUSE I HAVE A PLANE TO CATCH! HEAR ME?

Al took the first load to the elevator.

WOO-HOO! WE'RE FINALLY GOING! CAN YOU BELIEVE IT?

YOU KNOW WHAT? I'M ACTUALLY EXCITED ABOUT THIS!

I MEAN IT. I REALLY AM.

While waiting for Al to return...

HOW 'BOUT GIVIN' ME A LITTLE INTRO THERE, JESSIE?

INTRODUCING THE HIGH RIDIN'EST COWBOY AROUND.

YOU FORGOT ROOTIN' TOOT-IN'EST!

THE HIGH RIDIN'EST ROOTIN' TOOTIN'EST COWBOY HERO OF ALL TIME, SHERIFF WOODY!

the Roundup Gang decided to play!

YEAH!
HOO-WEE!
SAY, LITTLE MISSIE, YOU NOTICE ANY *TROUBLE* AROUND THESE PARTS?
NARY A BIT. NOT WITH *SHERIFF WOODY* AROUND!
They went on playing...
NOW, WHERE'S MY TRUSTY STEED, *BULLSEYE?*
I HAVE TO RIDE OFF INTO THE SUNSET!
WHAT'S *HAPPENING?*
*IT'S WOODY!*
IT'S HORRIBLE! THEY'RE *TORTURING* HIM!
From the air duct, the toys could hear Woody!
I'M BEGGING YOU! I'M BEGGING YOU, STOP! *PLEASE!*
He was only being *tickled*.
WHAT ARE WE GOING TO DO, BUZZ?
USE YOUR *HEAD!*
*STOP! PLEASE!*

BUT I DON'T WANNA USE MY HEAD!

CHA-A-A-A-A-RGE!

WHAT'S GOING ON HERE?

BUZZ! GUYS! HEY, HOW DID YOU FIND ME?

WE'RE HERE TO *SPRING* YOU!

New Buzz grabbed Woody...

FELLAS! YOU DON'T UNDERSTAND! THESE ARE MY FRIENDS! BUZZ, PUT ME DOWN!

ALL RIGHT! LET'S GO!

SPACE RANGER

LIGHTYEAR

RETREAT!

when suddenly...

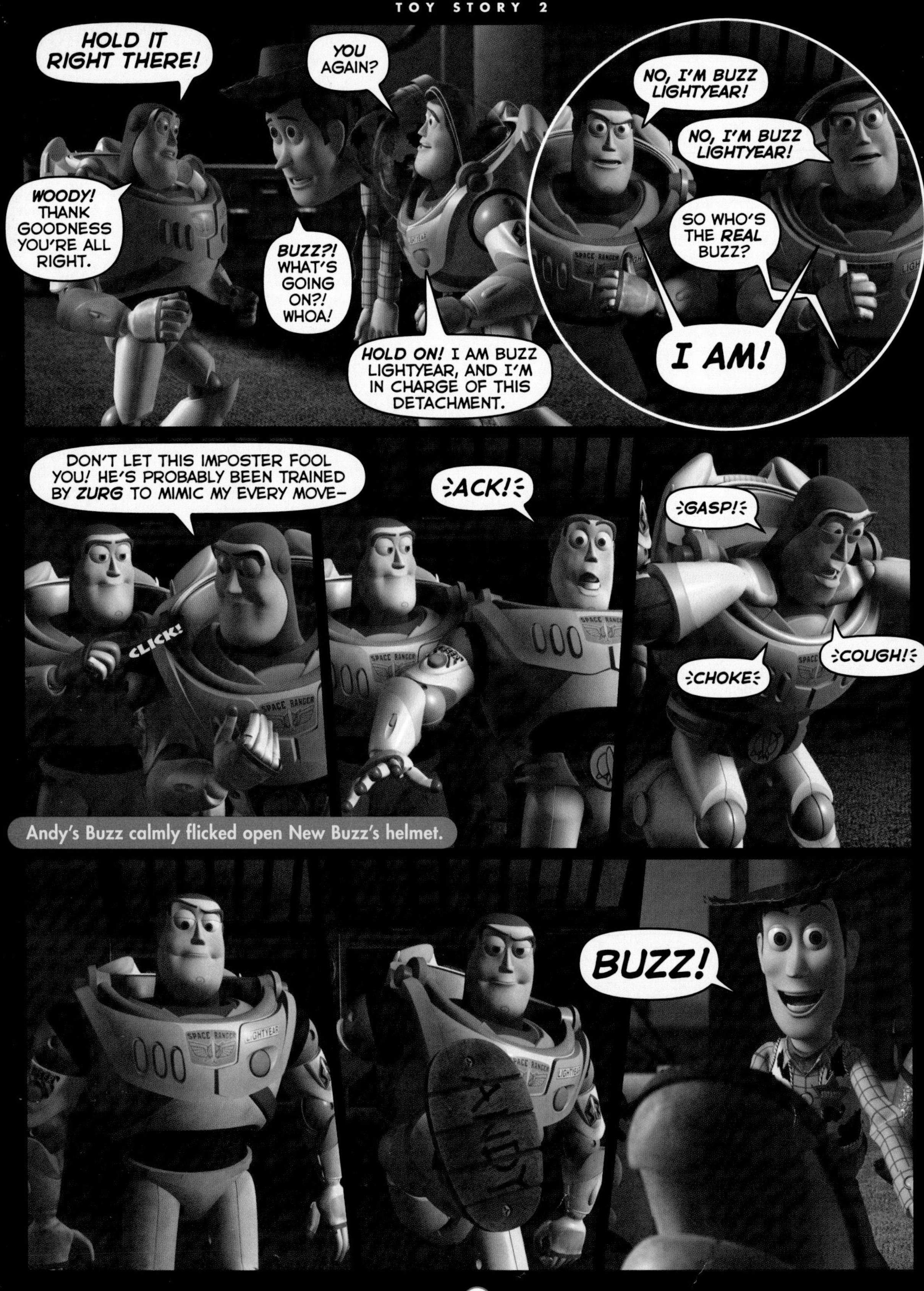


Andy's Buzz calmly flicked open New Buzz's helmet.

IT'S ALL RIGHT, SPACE RANGER. IT'S A CODE 546.
GASP YOU MEAN IT'S A—
YES.
AND HE'S A—
OH, YEAH.
LIGHTYEAR
YOUR MAJESTY.
WOODY, AL'S SELLING YOU TO A TOY MUSEUM, IN JAPAN!
WOODY, YOU'RE IN DANGER HERE. WE NEED TO LEAVE. NOW!
IT'S OKAY, BUZZ. I ACTUALLY WANT TO GO TO THE MUSEUM.
SEE, I'M A RARE SHERIFF WOODY DOLL, AND THESE GUYS ARE MY ROUNDUP GANG. IT'S THIS GREAT OLD TV SHOW AND I WAS THE STAR!
AND THERE WAS ALL THIS MERCHANDISE— YOU SHOULDA SEEN IT! THERE WAS A RECORD PLAYER, AND A YO-YO. BUZZ, I WAS A YO-YO!
WAS?
THIS IS WEIRDIN' ME OUT.

WOODY, STOP THIS NONSENSE AND LET'S GO!
AH, BUZZ. SIGH.
I CAN'T GO. I CAN'T ABANDON THESE GUYS!
THEY NEED ME TO GET INTO THIS MUSEUM. WITHOUT ME THEY'LL GO BACK INTO STORAGE— MAYBE FOREVER.
WOODY, YOU'RE NOT A COLLECTOR'S ITEM! YOU'RE A CHILD'S PLAYTHING!
YOU—ARE— A—TOY!
FOR HOW MUCH LONGER? ONE MORE RIP AND ANDY'S DONE WITH ME.
WHAT DO I DO THEN, BUZZ, HUH? YOU TELL ME!
SOMEWHERE IN THAT PAD OF STUFFING IS A TOY WHO TAUGHT ME THAT LIFE'S ONLY WORTH LIVING IF YOU'RE BEING LOVED BY A KID. AND I TRAVELED ALL THIS WAY TO RESCUE THAT TOY BECAUSE I BELIEVED IN HIM.
WELL, YOU WASTED YOUR TIME.
I DON'T HAVE A CHOICE, BUZZ. THIS MUSEUM— IT'S MY ONLY CHANCE.
TO DO WHAT, WOODY? WATCH CHILDREN FROM BEHIND GLASS AND NEVER BE LOVED AGAIN?
SOME LIFE.
LET'S GO, EVERYONE. HE'S NOT COMING WITH US.

Woody's ROUNDUP
PULL STRING - 9 DIFFERENT SAYINGS
GOOD GOING, WOODY. I THOUGHT THEY'D NEVER LEAVE.
WOODY?
JUST REMEMBER... YOU GOT A FRIEND IN ME...
YOU'VE GOT A FRIEND IN ME...

YOU'VE GOT TROUBLES, AND I'VE GOT 'EM, TOO...THERE ISN'T ANYTHING I WOULDN'T DO FOR YOU...
WE'LL STICK TOGETHER, AND WE'LL SEE IT THROUGH, 'CAUSE YOU'VE GOT A FRIEND IN ME.
WHAT AM I DOING???
YOU'RE RIGHT, PROSPECTOR. I CAN'T STOP ANDY FROM GROWING UP, BUT I WOULDN'T MISS IT FOR THE WORLD.
W-WOODY? WHERE ARE YOU GOING?
GASP!

BUZZ! BUZZ! I'M COMING WITH YOU!
WAIT! I'LL BE BACK IN JUST A SECOND!
HEY, YOU GUYS! COME WITH ME! ANDY WILL PLAY WITH ALL OF US. I KNOW IT! C'MON, JESSIE! THIS IS WHAT IT'S ALL ABOUT–MAKING A CHILD HAPPY! AND YOU KNOW IT!
I-I-I DON'T KNOW. I–

He sure was! Prospector was tightening the screws on Woody's escape route!

Before Woody could say another word, Al came in and packed up the Roundup Gang.
BZZZZ
HURRY! I CAN HEAR THE ELEVATOR!
As they returned to the elevator shaft, a dark figure appeared atop the rising lift.
IT'S ZURG!
GASP!
WATCH OUT! HE'S GOT AN ION BLASTER!
SO WE MEET AGAIN, BUZZ LIGHTYEAR... FOR THE LAST TIME!
New Buzz dove out of the way!
POW!
QUICK! GET ON THE EMERGENCY HATCH!
BZZZAAAP!
While Zurg and New Buzz traded fire, the other toys started jumping onto the elevator.

Zurg's blasts were getting closer and Buzz's laser wasn't working!
He needed another weapon.
AARGH!
Z-I-I-I-I-NG!
CRUNCH!
SURRENDER, BUZZ LIGHTYEAR. I HAVE WON.
UUH!
I'LL NEVER GIVE IN. YOU KILLED MY FATHER!
Zurg was too quick!

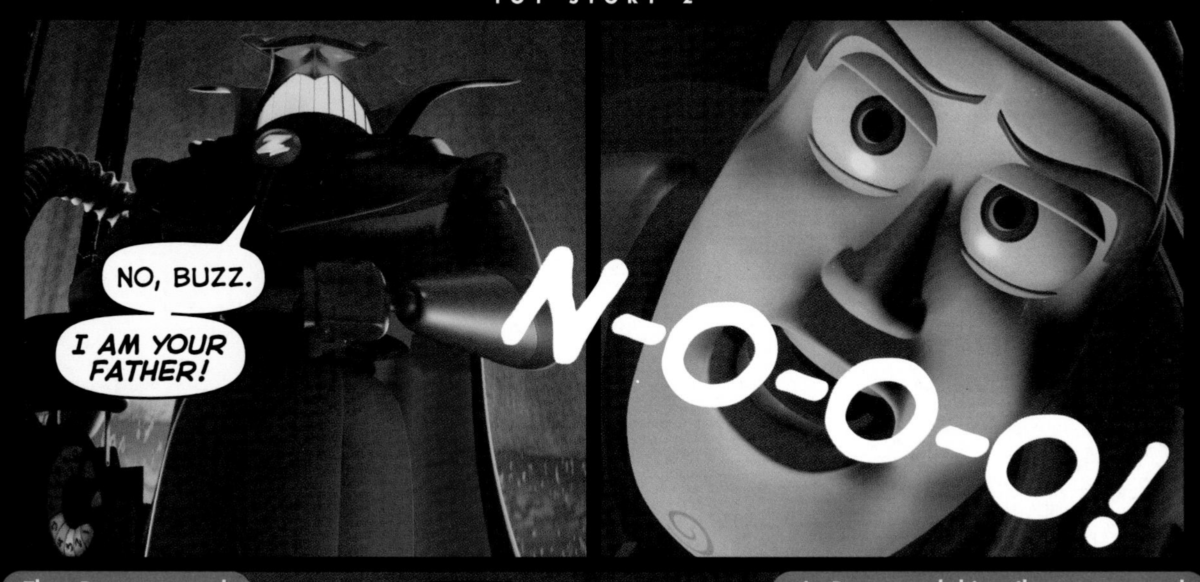


Then Rex appeared.

*BUZZ!* YOU COULD'VE DEFEATED ZURG ALL ALONG. YOU JUST NEED TO *BELIEVE* IN YOURSELF!

*PREPARE TO DIE.*

*AH! I CAN'T LOOK!*

As Rex turned, his tail swung around.

AAAAAAAHHHHHHHHH

I *DID* IT!

*I FINALLY DEFEATED ZURG!*

*FATHER!*

Meanwhile, Andy's Buzz and the toys were desperately trying to rescue Woody.
!!!
C'MON! C'MON!
And they almost had him!
AHH, FINALLY!
But Slink couldn't hang on!
Outside, as Al drove away, the toys came upon a familiar sight.
!?!
HOW ARE WE GONNA GET HIM NOW?
PIZZA, ANYONE?

BUZZ, ARE YOU COMING?
NO...
I HAVE A LOT OF CATCHING UP TO DO WITH MY *DAD.*

Zurg was back!
GOOD, SON.

POW!
NOW, GO LONG!
A kinder, gentler Zurg.

?!?
I'M GETTIN' IT. *YIPPEE!*

FAREWELL.

Buzz—Andy's Buzz—took control of the Pizza Planet truck.
*HAMM AND POTATO HEAD, OPERATE THE LEVERS AND KNOBS!*
*SLINK, TAKE THE PEDALS.*
*REX, YOU NAVIGATE!*
SPACE RANGER LIGHTYEAR

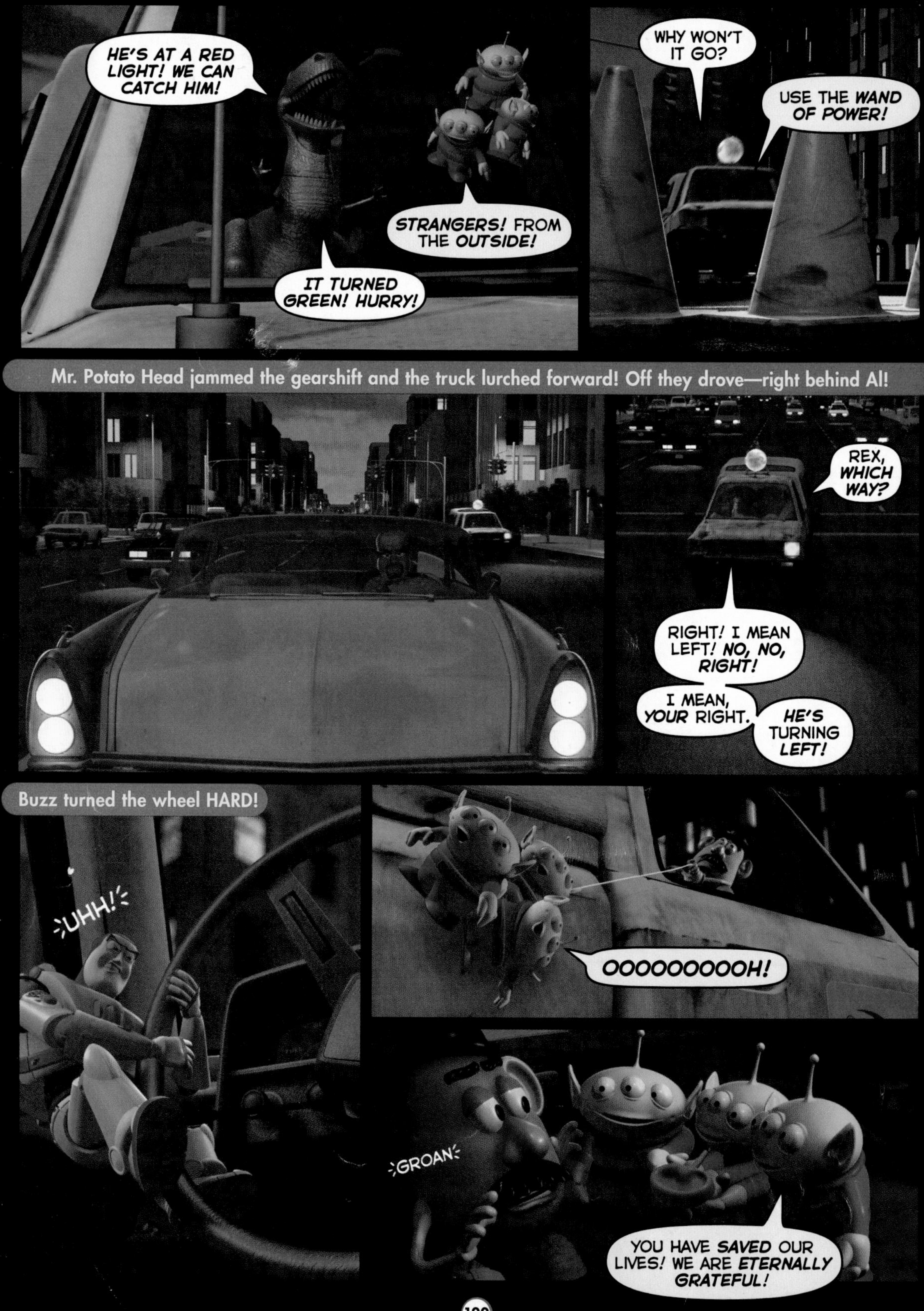

HE'S AT A RED LIGHT! WE CAN CATCH HIM!

STRANGERS! FROM THE OUTSIDE!

IT TURNED GREEN! HURRY!

WHY WON'T IT GO?

USE THE WAND OF POWER!

Mr. Potato Head jammed the gearshift and the truck lurched forward! Off they drove—right behind Al!

Buzz turned the wheel HARD!

UHH!

OOOOOOOOOH!

GROAN

YOU HAVE SAVED OUR LIVES! WE ARE ETERNALLY GRATEFUL!

The airport...
FAR EAST
FAR EAST
GETAWAY AIR
YO
THERE HE IS!
FAR EAST
FLIGHT TO TOKYO DEPARTING FROM GATE B3.
Taking cover in a pet carrier, the toys pursued Al's bags down the luggage ramp.
ONCE WE GO THROUGH, WE JUST NEED TO FIND THAT CASE.
THE MYSTIC PORTAL! OOOOOOOOH!
THERE'S THE CASE!
NO, THERE'S THE CASE.
YOU TAKE THAT ONE, WE'LL TAKE THIS ONE!
WOODY?
AWWW, NICE FLASH, THOUGH!

Prospector jumped out and knocked Buzz off the conveyor belt.

As the toys came running, Prospector slashed Woody with his pick. He raised it for the final blow when...

The toys blinded Prospector with the flashes!

And sent him packing... in a kid's knapsack!

Prospector would be played with after all.

Just then...
HEY, GUYS! HELP US OUT HERE!
OH, NO! JESSIE!
RIDE LIKE THE WIND, BULLSEYE!
Jessie was still stuck in the case!

FAR EAST

Unable to reach Jessie in time, Woody snuck onto the plane.

In the plane's cargo bay...

EXCUSE ME, MA'AM, BUT I BELIEVE YOU'RE ON THE *WRONG FLIGHT*.
WOODY!

C'MON, JESS. IT'S TIME TO TAKE YOU *HOME*.

The luggage tram pulled away. The jet engines started, and the plane taxied down the runway.
VVRRRR
VVRRRR
THIS IS BAD.
YOU SURE ABOUT THIS?
YES! LET'S GO!
WOODY!
AHHH!
Buzz Lightyear... to the rescue!
BUZZ!
BUZZ, GET BEHIND THE WHEEL!
Woody swung his pull string like a lasso...

And lassoed a bolt on the landing gear.

JUST PRETEND IT'S THE FINAL EPISODE OF WOODY'S ROUNDUP!

JESSIE! LET GO!

WHAT? ARE YOU CRAZY?

IT WAS *CANCELED!* WE NEVER SAW IF YOU *MADE* IT!

YAAAAAAH!

THEN LET'S FIND OUT TOGETHER!

Woody yanked the pull string free just before the plane took off.

WE DID IT! WE DID IT! THAT WAS DEFINITELY WOODY'S FINEST HOUR!

NICE ROPIN', COWBOY.

YEEEEEE-HAAAAA!

VRRRRRRM!

LET'S GO HOME.

Poor Woody! His arm had ripped again!

When Andy finally came home...
HEY, WOODY!
WOODY! OH, WOW! NEW TOYS! COOL! THANKS, MOM!
GOOD THING I DIDN'T BRING HIM TO COWBOY CAMP. HIS WHOLE ARM MIGHT'VE COME OFF.
WELCOME Home ANDY
DADDY!
OH, NO.
Later, Woody's arm was repaired once more, Wheezy got a new squeaker...
I FEEL A SONG COMING ON!
YOU'VE GOT A FRIEND IN ME...
and Jessie and Bullseye got a brand-new family.
STILL WORRIED?
ABOUT ANDY? NAH! IT'LL BE FUN WHILE IT LASTS.
BESIDES, WHEN IT ALL ENDS, I'LL HAVE OL' BUZZ LIGHTYEAR TO KEEP ME COMPANY...FOR INFINITY AND BEYOND.
THE END